Award-winning author

Rebecca Winters

is known and loved for her unique characters
and intense, deeply emotional stories.
Here is just some of the praise her books have received....

"Rebecca Winters' latest is full of emotional scenes,
fantastic characterization and endearing romance."
—*Romantic Times* on *His Very Own Baby*

"Winters weaves a magical spell that is unforgettable,"
—*Affaire de Coeur* on *The Nutcracker Prince*

"An emotionally intense premise...
dynamic characters, heartrending scenes
and wonderful romance."
—*Romantic Times* on *Undercover Baby*

Look out in Harlequin Romance® in June for

His Majesty's Marriage (#3705)
by
Lucy Gordon and Rebecca Winters

Harlequin Romance®
is delighted to invite you to

WHITE WEDDINGS

It's the countdown to the Big Day: the guests are invited,
the flowers are arranged, the dress is ready and the sparks
between the lucky couple are sizzling hot....
Only, our blushing bride and groom-to-be have yet
to become "engaged" in the bedroom!

Is it choice or circumstance keeping their passions
in check? Read our brand-new miniseries
WHITE WEDDINGS to find out why a very modern bride
wears white on her wedding day!

Look out in May for

Emma's Wedding (#3699)
by
BETTY NEELS

Readers are invited to visit Rebecca Winters's Web site
at www.rebeccawinters-author.com.

THE BRIDEGROOM'S VOW

Rebecca Winters

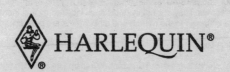

HARLEQUIN®

TORONTO • NEW YORK • LONDON
AMSTERDAM • PARIS • SYDNEY • HAMBURG
STOCKHOLM • ATHENS • TOKYO • MILAN • MADRID
PRAGUE • WARSAW • BUDAPEST • AUCKLAND

My story takes place in Greece, a country of incredible
history and beauty. My favorite living artist,
Thomas McKnight, fell in love with Greece, too.
He has created one masterpiece after another
of Mykonos, Chora, Kalafati, the Aegean and much,
much more. It is to him and his wife, Renate,
that I dedicate this book.

ISBN 0-373-03693-0

THE BRIDEGROOM'S VOW

First North American Publication 2002.

Copyright © 2001 by Rebecca Winters.

Visit us at www.eHarlequin.com

Printed in U.S.A.

CHAPTER ONE

DIMITRIOS heard footsteps in the passage outside his door. It was the middle of the night. Curious to know what was going on, he flung his covers aside and hurried out into the hall.

"Leon?" he whispered when he saw his adored elder brother carrying a suitcase. "What's happening?"

Leon spun around. "Go back to bed, Dimi."

Ignoring the command, he rushed up to Leon. "Where are you going?"

"Lower your voice. You'll find out soon enough."

"But you can't just leave!" He worshipped Leon who'd been father, brother and protector all rolled into one this last year. "Wherever you have to go, I'll come with you. I can be ready in two minutes."

"No, Dimi. You have to stay here with Uncle Spiros and our cousins. I should be back in a week."

Tears filled his eyes. "The cousins aren't fun like you, and Uncle Spiros is too strict."

"Since our parents died, he's been good to us in his own way, Dimi. It won't be so bad."

Panic-stricken, Dimitrios threw his arms around Leon, trying to prevent him from leaving. "Please let me come with you."

"You can't. You see, I'm getting married before the night's out. It's all been arranged."

Married?

Dimitrios felt like his world had come to an end. "Which one of your girlfriends is it?"

"Ananke Paulos."

"I've never heard of her. Will you bring her here?"

"No," he said on a heavy sigh. "We'll be living in our parents' villa."

"Then I'll come and live with you. I can sleep in my old room like always."

He shook his head. "I'm sorry, Dimi. A woman likes her own house."

"But that means you and I'll never live together again!"

"Hey—we'll always be brothers. I'll visit you every day, and you'll come to visit us."

The pain kept getting worse. "Do you love her more than me?" His voice wobbled.

Leon stared down at him with eyes full of anguish. Dimitrios didn't know his brother could look like that. It terrified him.

"Not at all. In fact I would give anything in the world if I didn't have to marry her. But she's pregnant with my child."

Dimitrios blinked in astonishment.

"She's going to have your baby?"

"Yes."

"You made a baby with a woman you don't love?" He couldn't comprehend such a thing.

"Oh, Dimi—listen to me. You're only twelve, not quite old enough for a man's feelings to have taken over inside you yet. When that day comes, your body will react when you see a beautiful woman. You'll want to hold her, make love to her. The pleasure a woman can bring you is to die for.''

Dimitrios frowned through the tears. "To die for?"

A sound of frustration came out of Leon. "I only mean that when a man and a woman make love, it's wonderful beyond your imagination.''

"Was it that way with Ananke?"

"Yes."

"But if you don't love her?"

"You can feel great desire for a woman without loving her. I would never have married her but for the baby. Now I have to do my duty as a Pandakis.''

"No, you don't!" Dimitrios cried from the depths of his soul. "What kind of a woman would want to live with you if she knew you didn't love her?"

A groan escaped Leon's throat. "Dimi? There are other reasons she wants to marry me.''

"What reasons?"

"Money, status.''

"I don't understand.''

"You know our family has run a successful financial empire in Greece for generations. Our reputation is known throughout the corporate world. Uncle Spiros meets with important, influential people, just like our father did before he died.

"That's the reason Ananke tricked me. She was hoping to have my baby so she could belong to our family. Now she's going to get her wish, but it won't be the wedding she imagined. We're going to be married at the church by the priest with no one there but her grandmother to watch.''

"I hate her!" Dimitrios blurted in fresh pain.

"Don't say that, Dimi. After tonight she'll be part of our family."

"I *will* say it!" With tears streaming down his face, Dimitrios backed away from his brother. "Do you think our mother married our father because of his money?"

Dimitrios had to wait a long time to hear a response.

"Probably."

Leon was always brutally honest. His answer crushed Dimitrios. Sick with grief over what his brother had just told him, he said, "Can't a rich man find a woman who will love him for himself?"

"I don't know the answer to that question. The point is, I don't want you to make the same mistake I did. Unfortunately that's where you've got a problem."

"What do you mean?"

"One day you'll be the head of the Pandakis Corporation because Uncle Spiros says you've got the smartest head on your shoulders of anyone in the family. You're also better looking than all the Pandakis men put together.

"You'll be able to have your pick of any woman in the world. They'll throw themselves at you. You, little brother, will have to be more careful than most men to make certain no woman gets pregnant with your baby and tricks you into marriage."

Dimitrios ground his teeth. "That will never happen to me."

Leon gave him a sad smile. "How do you know that?"

"I won't ever make love to a woman. Then I won't have to worry."

"Of course you will." He tousled Dimitrios's curly

black hair. "We'll continue this conversation next week when I take us hiking."

Dimitrios watched his brother disappear around the corner of their uncle's villa. It was just like the night a year ago when they learned that their parents had been killed. Dimitrios had wanted to die then, too.

Alexandra Hamilton didn't trust anyone to dye her hair except Michael at the Z-Attitude hair salon in her home town of Paterson, New Jersey.

He was a genius at his craft. That went without saying. But more to the point, she trusted him with secrets the way she would a father confessor.

Today he was wearing his hair in blue spikes. Michael wasn't a mere coiffeur par excellence. He entertained everyone who flocked to his busy salon. Women adored him, young and old.

Her green eyes met his in the huge mirror with its border of stage lights.

"When are you going to emerge from this boring brown chrysalis and reveal your natural blond mane to *his* wondrous gaze?"

"Not until *he* falls in love with me as I am."

He meaning Dimitrios Pandakis, of course. Alex loved him with every fiber of her being.

"I hate to tell you this, but you've been saying that ever since you went to work for his company. Four years now, isn't it?"

Alex stuck her tongue out at him.

"Sorry," he said in the most unrepentant voice she'd ever heard.

Her softly rounded chin lifted a good inch. "I'm making progress."

"You mean since you slipped a little poison into his private secretary's coffee six months ago?"

"*Michael!* That's not funny. She was a wonderful woman. I still miss her and know he does, too."

"Just kidding. I thought the trip to China went without a hitch."

"It did. He gave me another bonus."

"That makes quite a few. He'd better be careful or he might just find himself on the losing end of a very clever takeover orchestrated by none other than his own Ms. Hamilton." A devilish expression broke out on Michael's face. "Are you still making him call you that?"

She tried to hide her smile. "Yes."

"It gives you great pleasure, doesn't it."

"*Extreme.* I must be the only woman on seven continents who doesn't fall all over him trying to get his attention."

"Yes, and it shows."

"What it *does* is make me different from all the other women," she defended. "One day he's going to take notice."

"Let's hope it happens before he marries one of his own kind to produce an heir who'll inherit his fortune. He's not getting any younger, you know."

A familiar pain pierced her heart. "Thank you for playing on my greatest fear."

"But you love me anyway for telling you the truth."

She bit her lip. "He has a nephew he loves like a son. Mrs. Landau once told me Dimitrios's brother died, so he took over the guardianship of his nephew. There's this look he gets on his face whenever Leon calls him from Greece."

"Well, then—" He fastened her hair in a secure twist. "I guess you have no worries he's anxious to start a family of his own."

"Oh, stop!"

He grinned, eyeing her from the darkened roots of her head to the matronly black shoes she wore on her feet.

"Only your hairdresser knows for sure. I must say I did a good job when I transformed you."

"It doesn't suit you to be modest, Michael. Why not admit you created a masterpiece."

Thanks to his expertise in doing hair and makeup for a lot of his friends in the theater, he'd come up with a disguise that made her look like a nondescript secretary much older than her twenty-five years.

"Possibly," he quipped. "However, I may have gone too far when I suggested those steel-rimmed glasses you wear. You could walk on the set of a World War Two film being produced as we speak and fit right in."

"That's been the idea all along. You know I'm indebted to you." She handed him a hundred-dollar bill, which he refused.

"We worked out a deal, remember? In return for some free hair appointments, my friends and I get to stay free at your hotel suite in Thessalonica during the fair."

She shook her head. "I've been thinking about it and have decided I'm getting the better end of that deal."

He wiggled his eyebrows. "Do you even know how much a suite in that place costs for *one* night?"

"No."

"I guess you don't have to know when you're the private secretary of Dimitrios Pandakis. Oh, if the rest of the world had any idea how you really live these days," he said dramatically.

"You know I don't care about that."

His expression grew serious for a moment. "Is it really worth it to be the bridesmaid, but never the bride?"

He'd touched a painful nerve and knew it. "I can't imagine not seeing him every day."

"You're hopeless, darling."

"Tell me about it." She got out of the chair and gave him a kiss on the cheek. "See you in Greece next week."

"We're coming as Mysian troubadours. Are you sure I can't bring you a costume along with his? There's this marvelous gold affair—Italian renaissance. I can borrow it from the opera company."

She shook her head. "Ms. Hamilton doesn't do costumes. It's not in her character."

"Pity."

Alex chuckled. "Have a safe trip over, Michael."

"You mean with three hundred of us on our charter flight squashed like Vienna sausages in the can? Lucky you, riding in the Pandakis private jet."

"I'll admit that part's nice. Bye for now."

She left the salon, grateful that the disguise Michael had created for her had worked perfectly during the four years she'd been in Dimitrios's employ. She'd won the man's confidence. But the thought that it was all she might ever win from him wasn't to be considered.

As for her other fear, it was foolish to worry that when she arrived in Greece, Giorgio Pandakis might recognize her from the past. Not when Dimitrios had never shown any signs of remembering.

Nine years was too long a time for a man who'd been drunk to recall accosting an unsuspecting sixteen-year-old girl. Thankfully someone had been outside the silk museum in Paterson that night looking for him and had heard her screams.

Alex could still see her protector's face as it had appeared in the shadowy moonlight. Like a dark, avenging prince, Dimitrios Pandakis himself had pulled his cousin off her before knocking him to the ground, unconscious.

Assisting her to her feet, he'd told her he would help her press charges if she wanted him to. Alex, who stood there on trembling legs thankful for deliverance, had been shocked that he would defend an anonymous teenage girl over his cousin.

Dimitrios didn't accuse her of encouraging the situation. He didn't try to pay her off. He showed no fear of the scandal that would naturally ensue once her father heard about it. With a name as famous as Pandakis, that kind of news would make headlines. Yet he'd been willing to put his family through embarrassment for her sake.

In that moment, she loved him.

Once her sobs began to subside, she assured him it wouldn't be necessary to call in the police. He'd come to her rescue before things had gone too far. All she wanted was to forget it had ever happened.

After thanking him again for saving her, she ran off across the garden to her house, clutching the torn pieces of the silk blouse to her chest.

Just before she disappeared around the corner, she

watched him throw his loathsome cousin over his shoulder with the ease only a tall, powerful man possessed.

Her green eyes stayed fastened on him until she couldn't see the outline of his silhouette any longer. But even if he'd gone, the man was unforgettable.

By the time she climbed into bed that night she determined that one day, when she was older, they would meet again. It would be under vastly different circumstances, of course. And no matter what it took, she'd make certain he found her unforgettable, too.

As Dimitrios buttoned his shirt, he heard a rap on his bedroom door. Assuming it was Serilda, the housekeeper who'd been like a favorite aunt since he was a little boy, he told her to come in.

The door opened, but the usual burst of information about the weather and the state of the world wasn't forthcoming.

Unless she'd sent a maid to him with coffee and rolls, it wouldn't be anyone else but his nephew.

Dimitrios felt great love for the twenty-two-year old whose build and mannerisms were a constant reminder of Leonides Pandakis, Dimitrios's deceased elder brother.

By some miracle, his pregnant bride survived the car crash that took Leonides's life on their honeymoon. Their unborn child, christened Leon at birth, had also been spared.

Like his father, he was a happy boy with a friendly, outgoing nature. A typical teen with his share of problems, he'd survived those years and had grown into a fine young man who was halfway through his university studies and showed a healthy enthusiasm for life. Or so Dimitrios had thought.

But since Dimitrios's return from China yesterday, he'd seen a big change in his nephew. Normally Leon sought his company at the slightest opportunity, giving him chapter and verse of anything and everything happening in his world.

This time he'd only greeted his uncle with a hug, then disappeared from the villa without a word of explanation. It was totally unlike him. Dimitrios had glimpsed shadows in the brown eyes he'd inherited from his mother.

Something was wrong, of course. He hoped it wasn't serious. Maybe now he'd find out.

"You're up early, Leon," he called to him. "That's good because I was about to come and find you. I've missed you and have been looking forward to one of our talks."

After shrugging into his suit jacket, he emerged from his walk-in closet, hoping his nephew would reveal whatever had been troubling him. But when he discovered it was Ananke still in her nightgown and robe who'd crossed his threshold uninvited, revulsion rose like bile in his throat.

He'd always felt a natural antipathy toward the woman who'd tricked his brother into marriage, and never more than at this moment. Yet love for his brother's son had tempered that destructive emotion enough for him to tolerate her presence in the villa while acting as guardian to young Leon.

Plastic surgery had removed all traces of the scars on her forehead left by the accident. Would that it could as easily erase the scars in Dimitrios's heart. But nothing could take away the memory of a mercenary female who'd lured Leon to her bed for the express purpose of begetting a Pandakis. Because of her, his brother was dead.

Back then Ananke had been a precocious eighteen-year-old, aware of her assets and how to use them. Now she was a forty-one-year-old female, only six years older than Dimitrios. A woman most men found attractive, yet she showed no interest in them.

Not for the first time had he wondered if she was hoping to become *his* bride. Though she'd let it be known to family and friends that she refused to consider marriage until she saw her son settled down with a wife of his own, Dimitrios knew it was an excuse to stay on at the villa. No other man could offer her the Pandakis lifestyle.

At a recent family birthday party, his cousin Vaso had speculated with similar thoughts to him. Dimitrios's eyes must have reflected his abhorrence of the subject because the eldest of Spiros Pandakis's sons didn't broach it again.

Unfortunately nothing seemed to slake Ananke's ambition. Her temerity in seeking him out in a place as private as his own bedroom at seven in the morning gave him proof that she had few scruples left.

Out of love for his brother and nephew, he'd treated her with civility all these years. Regrettably this morning she'd stepped over a forbidden line and would know his wrath.

"You have no right to be in this part of the villa, Ananke."

"Please don't be angry with me. I have to talk to you

before Leon finds you.'' She looked like she'd been crying. ''This is important.''

''Important enough to put false ideas in the minds of the staff, let alone my nephew?'' he demanded in a quiet rage. ''From here on out, if you have something to say to me in private, call me at my office.''

''Wait,'' she cried as he swept past her and strode down the corridor toward the entrance to the villa, impervious to her pleading.

''Dimi!'' She half-sobbed his nickname in an effort to detain him.

The use of the endearment only his parents and brother had ever called him had the effect of corrosive acid being poured into a wound that would never heal.

Compared to the sound of his ever-lengthening footsteps, the rapid patter of her sandals while she tried to catch up with him made the odd cadence on the marble tiles. To his relief, the patter finally faded.

He'd just shut the front door and had headed for the parking area around the side of the villa when Leon called to him.

Dimitrios wheeled around, surprised to discover his nephew following him.

''Uncle.'' He ran up. ''I need to talk to you. *Alone*,'' he added in a confiding voice. ''Would you let me drive you to the office?''

For a fleeting moment Dimitrios felt guilty for dismissing Ananke. She had obviously been trying to alert him to something. But when he considered her reckless actions, which would be misconstrued by his staff no matter how loyal they were to him, he wasn't sorry he'd cut her off.

Years ago Leonides had married Ananke to do the honorable thing and give his child the Pandakis name. After his brother died, Dimitrios determined no breath of scandal would ever touch his nephew if he could help it.

Of course Leon was a free agent, capable of getting into trouble on his own—*if* that were the case. Under the circumstances, Dimitrios knew he wouldn't be able to concentrate on business until he'd learned what was plaguing his nephew.

"Work can wait. Why don't we take a drive and stop somewhere for lunch. I'll call Stavros and tell him I won't be in until afternoon."

"You're sure you wouldn't rather spend time with one of your women friends now that you're back from China?"

"No woman is more important than you, Leon."

"Are you sure? When I was at Elektra the other night, Ionna went out of her way to ask me when you were coming home. She said it was urgent that she talk to you. She even asked me for your cell phone number, but I told her I didn't remember it."

Dimitrios shook his head. "If she was that forward with you, then she has written her own death sentence."

His nephew eyed him steadily. "She's very beautiful."

"I agree, but you know my rule, Leon. When a woman starts to take the initiative, I move on."

"I think it's a good rule. I've been using it, too, and I must say it works."

For some strange reason, the admission didn't sit well with Dimitrios. It sounded too cynical for Leon.

"To be frank, I'm glad you'd rather be with me this morning," came the emotional response.

Dimitrios gave his nephew a hug. Minutes later their car was headed into the hills of Thessalonica overlooking the bay. While Leon drove, Dimitrios checked in with his assistant.

"Stavros? Can you spare me for a few hours longer?"

"The truth?"

His question surprised Dimitrios.

"Always."

"Ms. Hamilton and I may work an ocean apart, but since she became your private secretary, I've begun to feel superfluous."

"You're indispensable to the company, Stavros. You know that," he rushed to assure him. The sixty-six-year-old man had kept the Greek end of the Pandakis Corporation running smoothly for decades.

Ms. Hamilton, the understudy of his former private secretary in New York until Mrs. Landau's unexpected passing, was a six-month-old enigma, still in her infancy. Yet Dimitrios could understand why Stavros made the remark.

In a word, she was a renaissance woman. Brilliant. Creative. A combination of a workaholic and efficiency expert who, though she was no great beauty, happened to be blessed with a pleasant nature. She was many things—too many, in fact, to put a label on her. Mrs. Landau had known what she was doing when she'd hired her.

Before their trip to China, Dimitrios had wondered how he'd ever gotten along without her. During their week's stay in Beijing while he'd watched her weave her magic before their inscrutable colleagues with the finesse of a statesman, he finally figured it out.

She had a woman's mind for detail, but she thought like a man. Best of all for Dimitrios, she had no interest in him.

"Ms. Hamilton brings her own genius to the company, just as you brought yours many years ago and tutored me, Stavros. I'm looking forward to next week when the two of you meet for the first time. She holds you in great reverence, you know."

"I, too, shall enjoy making the acquaintance of this American paragon. Spring greets Winter."

"Since she's in her late thirties, it would be more accurate to say summer, and you're sounding uncharacteristically maudlin, Stavros."

"You have to allow me the vicissitudes of my age."

Dimitrios chuckled, but beneath the banter he could sense his assistant's vulnerability. Perhaps a word in Ms. Hamilton's ear that she leave something important for Stavros to handle for the fair would help.

"Just so we understand each other, I won't allow you to retire until I do. See you later this afternoon."

"What's wrong with Stavros?" his nephew asked as he clicked off the phone.

Putting his head back to relax, Dimitrios murmured, "He's suddenly aware of growing older."

"I know how he feels."

Dimitrios would have laughed if Leon hadn't sounded so serious. "You said you wanted to talk. Since you brought up Ionna, I have to wonder if you're not about to tell me you've fallen for a girl your mother doesn't like."

Leon shook his head. "That's not why we argued. I told her I dislike my business classes and want to drop out of the university. It's only September. I can still withdraw without penalty before the fall semester starts in three weeks."

Dimitrios schooled himself not to react. "To feel that strongly, you must have a very good reason."

"My heart isn't in it!" he cried. "I don't think it ever was. Mother's always had this vision of me taking my place in the family corporation. She says I owe it to my father's memory. But business doesn't appeal to me. Do you think that makes me some sort of traitor?" he asked in an anxious voice.

"Of course not," Dimitrios scoffed.

At this point he could have told his nephew a few home truths. Like the fact that Leon's father hadn't been interested in the family business, either.

There was information Leon didn't know about his mother that would shed more light on her determination to make certain he held onto his birthright.

But Dimitrios's hands were tied, because telling his nephew the truth about the past would hurt him more than it would help.

"What do you want to do with your life, or do you even know yet?"

His nephew heaved a sigh. "It's just an idea, but it's grown stronger with every visit to Mount Athos."

Mount Athos.

"You took me there the first time. Remember? We did a walking tour, and ate and slept at the various monasteries."

Yes. He remembered. Especially his nephew's fascination with the monks...

Dimitrios straightened in the seat.

Like a revelation he knew what Leon was going to say before he said it.

"Uncle? Last night I told mother I'm thinking of entering an order. That's when she ran out of my bedroom in hysterics. I've never seen her react like that to anything. Would you talk to her about it? You're the only person she'll listen to."

Lord.

Was it possible that Leon's hero-worship of him had caused his nephew to dismiss a woman's love as unimportant?

Ananke's unprecedented visit to his bedroom this morning was beginning to make sense in a brand-new way.

Since the death of Leonides she'd lived on sufferance under Uncle Spiros's roof until his passing, then under the protection of Dimitrios.

If her son renounced all his worldly goods and went to live on a mountain, Ananke wouldn't only have lost a son to the church, she would have no choice but to move into a house Dimitrios would provide for her. A comfortable enough pied-à-terre befitting the widow of Leonides. All her dreams smashed.

"Before I say anything to your mother, I'd like to hear more about how *you* feel."

"As I said, I'm only thinking about it."

"Our trip to Mount Athos took place ten years ago. That's a long time to give a young man to think."

Leon blushed. The reaction tugged at Dimitrios's

heart. Perhaps his brother's son truly did have a vocation for the religious life. If it was the path he was meant to travel, far be it from Dimitrios to try to dissuade him.

Then again, like greener pastures, the monastic life might sound good to him because he was still young and lost.

Dimitrios had never questioned what direction his own life would go. He couldn't relate to Leon in that regard, but he *was* his guardian. As such, he felt it incumbent to listen as his nephew poured out his heart.

Afterward he would point out the ramifications of a decision that a twenty-two-year-old mind wasn't capable of envisioning yet. For one thing, it would break his mother's heart. Ananke might be many things, but she loved her son.

For another, it would destroy something inside Dimitrios if he thought his own tormented past had anything to do with the drastic step his nephew was contemplating.

Suddenly Dimitrios felt older than Stavros.

CHAPTER TWO

ALEX'S family always complained that she didn't stay long enough when she came to Paterson for visits. Her parents had never approved of her intentionally making herself look older in order to get hired by the Pandakis company. It was a sore point Alex argued with her mother every time they got together.

"Surely after four years you could start easing back to your normal self by lightening your hair in increments, wearing clothes that suit your age. I haven't seen my own daughter for so long, I don't remember what you look like."

"Mom..." Alex took a deep breath. "I wanted to be hired so badly, I would have done anything to gain Mrs. Landau's approval. I thought if I looked like a solid, more mature, dependable type, I'd have a better chance with her. Mr. Pandakis may have the reputation of being a womanizer, but he's totally professional with the staff at the office.

"But Mrs. Landau's not there anymore, darling. Now that you've taken over her duties, it seems to me you can start being our daughter again."

"You don't understand, Mom."

"Oh, but I do. You're not willing to risk anything that would prevent you from being around him. He's a man to turn any woman's head, and he has, especially yours."

"Yes," she admitted. "He's—"

"Bigger than life?" her mother preempted her. "I

know. He's the reason you've stopped dating and no longer have a social life.''

''I can't right now. But when the trade fair is over, he's taking a three week vacation. I've been ordered to do the same.''

''Which means all you'll do is mope around here waiting until you can be back with him.''

Her mother knew her too well.

''Alexandra? I've tried not to interfere in your life too much. But it's obvious to me you're in love with the man. Because of that you're blind to certain truths.''

Alex didn't want to hear them.

''Darling— Can't you see he's not normal?''

''You mean because he's not married with three or four children by now?'' she cried.

''Yes. He's a person who's been blessed with so many gifts, I think he got lost somewhere along the way.''

Alex shook her head emphatically. ''If you knew him, you'd never say such a thing.''

''I'm not talking about his business prowess. There's something in his makeup that isn't right. My guess is he was marred in childhood and it stunted his emotional growth.

''How else do you explain his inability to settle down with one woman? Or for that matter, why Mrs. Landau seemed to choose only plain women to work for him. He's simply not an ordinary sort. Don't you agree? Honestly?''

Tears prickled Alex's eyes. ''Yes,'' she whispered.

''Darling.'' Her mother put an arm around her. ''All I want is your happiness, but I'm afraid if you continue to work for him, he'll go on taking advantage of your generous nature and you'll never find joy in being a wife, or a mother.''

Alex broke down for a minute, then wiped her eyes. ''Mom? There's something I have to tell you. Maybe then you'll understand why I can't seem to let him go. I—I didn't apply for a job at the Pandakis Corporation by chance,'' she stammered.

''I suspected as much. When their people came to Paterson for the international silk seminar your grandfather hosted ten years ago, I remember the huge impact so many wealthy, dark-haired men made on everyone. Not a bad place to start a career for a girl right out of college.''

''Actually it was nine years ago.''

Her mother sent her a shrewd regard. ''What went on that night? Did Dimitrios Pandakis's wandering eye light on you? Did he tell you to come and see him when you were all grown up?''

''No!'' Alex cried out. ''If only it had happened like that, I wouldn't have been forced to resort to subterfuge. It was Giorgio Pandakis—''

In a torrent of words she explained what had gone on nine years earlier when Dimitrios had saved her from his cousin. After confiding everything she said, ''He was willing to stand by me, Mom. He offered to help me because that's the kind of man he is.''

''No wonder you fell in love with him,'' her mother murmured in a saddened voice. ''I've tried to imagine what hold he's had over you all this time. Everything you'd done since than has been with him in mind.''

''I've never been able to look at another man. I couldn't!''

''But what has it really gotten you except heartache?

This has to stop, darling. A teenage fantasy is one thing. But he's become your obsession. Surely if it was meant to be, he would have returned your feelings by now."

She knew her mother was right. Everyone was right. Michael. Her friend Yanni.

But the pain was killing her.

"I'm afraid for you to go to Greece with him. It can only put you on a more intimate footing with him without getting anything back in return."

"I know, but I *have* to go. I'm in charge of the trade fair."

"I realize that. Oh, Alexandra, you've gotten yourself in way too deep. I particularly don't like the idea of your being anywhere near his cousin. Obviously he'd caused trouble in their family long before he set eyes on you, otherwise your boss wouldn't have been so straightforward in dealing with the situation."

It had taken Alex a few years before she'd figured that out.

"Don't worry, Mom. Giorgio's been married a long time and has a family. Besides, I'm not a teenager anymore, and he wouldn't give me a second glance now."

Her mother stared at her with anxious eyes. "I'm not so sure of that. You may look older now, but you'll always be a beautiful girl. Even so, lies have a way of surfacing. How do you think Mr. Pandakis will react if he finds out you intentionally disguised yourself to get hired?"

"Literally speaking it was Mrs. Landau who gave me the job."

"You know what I mean."

Alex sucked in her breath. "I have no idea how he'd feel."

"Yes, you do. You've just told me he's an honorable man when it comes to business. Men like that expect honor in return. Mark my words, Alexandra. Every minute you're in his employ, you're playing with fire."

"Don't you think I know that?" she blurted in agony. "I—I've been giving it a lot of thought. Between you and Michael, I'm convinced that the only thing to do is resign."

"If you really mean that, then go to Greece. Do your job. Don't go near his family, then come straight home on the first available commercial flight and hand in your resignation. He'll have three weeks to find another secretary within the company to replace you."

"You're right," she whispered brokenly. "My assistant Charlene would give anything to have my job. As soon as I get back, I'll look for something around here."

"Promise?"

"Yes." She gave her mother another hug. "Kiss Daddy for me. I have to run."

"Call me as often as you can."

"Okay. I love you, Mom. Thanks for the advice."

"It's more than advice, darling. It's a warning."

Tears swamped Alex's cheeks as she left the house and drove off with those words ringing in her ears. All the way to New York she relived the conversation with her mother. The fissure had cracked open wide, wide, wide.

What a fool Alex had been. Four years had come and gone. She was still forgettable to Dimitrios.

But if he never gave her another thought after she left his employ, she was determined he'd remember the fruit of her labors.

For the last eight months she'd given the international

textile fair her all. She hoped it would make Greece the forerunner in establishing business relations on a global scale.

Before Mrs. Landau had passed away, she'd told Alex that Dimitrios had been asked to host the trade fair at the behest of the Greek government. They needed a name guaranteed to bring success.

It was a project dear to Alex's heart in more ways than one. She immediately went to work on it and received glowing praise from Mrs. Landau. But before the older woman could present the complete project to Dimitrios for his approval, she suffered a fatal heart attack at her home.

Her death affected everyone in the company, especially Dimitrios, who'd considered her his right hand away from Greece. Suddenly he was trying to do Mrs. Landau's work plus his own.

When he'd asked Alex to take over as best she could, she'd sensed he felt she was a lightweight who couldn't handle the enormous trade fair project along with her normal duties.

Fearing she'd miss the one big opportunity to make her mark, Alex rushed to assure him that she'd already worked out most of the details with Mrs. Landau. Whenever he gave the word, she would start implementing the plans.

She remembered that evening so clearly. Her mind's eye could see the way he lounged back in his swivel chair and unfastened his tie. Fatigue lines had darkened his attractive face whose shadowed jaw gave evidence that he'd been going too hard, traveling too much without proper rest.

He stared at her with incurious eyes, causing her heart

to plummet. Although he hadn't told her no, she realized he had little faith in her abilities to take on something of such vital importance.

"Have you ever been to Greece, Ms. Hamilton?"

"No, but I have a history degree."

In the uneasy silence that followed her response, she watched him rub his forehead as if he had a headache. No doubt he did and was barely holding on to his patience.

"Do you have something written up you can show me now, or do you need more time?"

She took a deep breath. "I'll get the portfolio out of my office and be right back."

Upon her return she asked if she could spread the materials out on his desk. He nodded.

The second she positioned the first twenty-by-twenty-four inch drawing in front of him, the complacency left his face. As he sat forward, his well-shaped black brows drew together.

"This isn't Athens." His voice trailed off.

"Was your heart set on it for the trade fair?"

Instead of answering her, he continued his perusal.

Swallowing hard she said, "That's a rendition of medieval Thessalonica during the great Byzantine fair held in the twelfth century. Everyone came—from Constantinople, Egypt, Phoenicia, the Peloponnese."

His head finally lifted. This time his eyes reminded her of twin black fires. "*You* drew this?"

"It's only a sketch. I thought because Thessalonica is your home, it would be exciting and fitting to recreate that same fair with colorful merchant booths and flags from every country participating. The whole city can get involved by providing local foods and drinks, everyone in native costume. Troubadours, music, dancing.

"Since it was the great cultural center then and still is today, I can't think of another place in Greece more appropriate to host a trade fair, certainly not one of this magnitude."

She placed a sketch of a closeup of the bay in front of him. "We could invite the countries around the Mediterranean and as far away as Scandinavia to bring their restored ships and anchor them here like they once did. Everyone can go aboard to see their wares.

"It will be like stepping back in time, but the products will be the latest in materials and textiles from around the world.

"We'll launch a massive ad campaign on the Internet with each country having its own Web page to list their products. I've already procured Web addresses. People who aren't able to attend can place orders.

"Think what it would mean economically to the Greek Island cottage industries for example, not to mention new world markets. Of course the pièce de résistance will be *this*." He hadn't interrupted her yet, so she whipped out her next drawing.

"Follow the silk road from Thessalonica to Soufli. At various points along the route, the delegations will set up their silk exhibits. Visits to the mulberry tree farm and the silk mansion in Soufli will be the highlight of the tour.

"The weather will be warm and perfect in September. Imagine the streets of Soufli lined with booths showing every stage from the secretions of the silkworm, to the silk thread ending up as a cravate or a gown.

"We'll woo the media ahead of time so there'll be a blitz that hits airwaves around the wor—"

"Ms. Hamilton." He cut in on her.

Her body broke out in a cold sweat. *He didn't like it.* Afraid to look at him, she said, "Yes?"

"What you've put together here is nothing short of sheer genius. In fact I'm having difficulty assimilating everything all at once."

Alex had been ready to pass out from disappointment. She still felt light-headed, except that now it was for an entirely different reason.

"Unfortunately none of this can happen without hotel space," he muttered. "Every place of lodging in Macedonia and Thrace should have been notified months ago in order to carry out such a fantastic plan."

"They were."

His dark head reared back in stunned surprise.

"In Athens and the surrounding regions, too. I also notified the head of all the businesses involved, the restaurants, the universities, the musicians' network, the transport services, port authorities, police, so they would set aside the time and plan ahead how to accommodate the huge crowds.

"I assume this is what it's like mobilizing for war, except that in this case everyone will enjoy the spoils of victory."

"Lord," she heard him whisper.

"It's a good thing we're talking about this tonight," she informed him. "The day after tomorrow is the final date for me to confirm or cancel everything without penalty.

"I've been waiting to discuss the fair with you until you'd recovered from Mrs. Landau's passing. She was extremely fond of you, too. It should please you to know that every contact person has assured me they wouldn't have held on this long for anyone but Dimitrios Pandakis. It's an honor to work for you.'' She had a struggle at the last to keep the emotion out of her voice.

In an unconscious gesture he raked his hands through the luxuriant black hair she longed to touch. "Here I was beginning to think you were perfect, Ms. Hamilton. Now I can see you're not above bribery to get what you want. For that flaw, you've won yourself a full evening of work that could take us well into the night.''

With those words he'd just given her the first taste of her heart's desire.

"While you arrange to have our dinner sent up, I'll cancel my plans to attend the symphony and we'll start again. I want to hear this from the beginning.

"Slowly this time. Detail by detail until I've picked that brilliant brain of yours. I can see I've also underestimated the value of your American university education. Did you study any languages?''

"My degree specialized in classical European history, so there were several classes I had to take in Latin and Greek.''

"You speak and understand Greek?'' He sounded incredulous.

"No. But since I came to work for your company I've been trying to do both with the help of a tutor.''

"Who?''

"A graduate student from Athens who lives in my apartment building. He trades me lessons for meals.''

"You cook, too?''

"Yanni's not particular.''

Alex couldn't remember Dimitrios ever smiling at her before now. *What a gorgeous man he was.*

"When you call downstairs, tell the kitchen to send a gallon of coffee with the food."

"Which brand of decaffeinated do you prefer?"

He lifted a sardonic brow. "Forget everything you learned from Mrs. Landau."

"You don't really mean that. I happen to know she had your very best interest at heart."

Once more his black eyes flashed fire. "You happen to know a lot more than I thought possible."

I sincerely hope so. Otherwise how will I ever become unforgettable to you?

More tears dripped down Alex's face as she remembered that evening with him. He'd loved her idea and had let her run with it. But nothing else had changed in the intervening months. Nothing personal.

Her mother was right about him not being normal. Even Alex knew it was time to give up. The trade fair would have to be her swan song.

Unless she died of pain first...

Dimitrios left his New York office with the morning newspaper under his arm and rode the elevator to the parking garage level of the building.

"Ms. Hamilton hasn't arrived yet?" he asked his driver who was waiting for them with the limo.

"I haven't seen her, Mr. Pandakis."

He checked his watch. No crime had been committed because it was a only few minutes past eight. It surprised him because she was the most punctual person he'd ever met.

At the end of work yesterday he'd told her he would

drop by her apartment on the way to the airport to pick her up. To his surprise she'd said it wouldn't be necessary because she'd be coming by the office early to take care of some last-minute business.

"Mr. Pandakis?"

Dimitrios turned in time to see one of the parking attendants approach him.

"Your secretary just called. She said she was running late and her friend would drive her straight to the airport."

He blinked. No doubt Ms. Hamilton had many friends, but the only one he'd ever heard about was Yanni. A compatriot.

Besides cooking him meals in exchange for language lessons, was she his pillow friend? It might explain why she'd chosen not to call Dimitrios on her cell phone to tell him about the change in plans. Particularly not if her tutor were lying next to her having a hard time saying goodbye.

The idea that Ms. Hamilton might have a love life made her more of an enigma than ever because she'd never let it interfere with her work. For quite some time he'd been aware that she wasn't like most women. That's why she'd become so valuable to him.

He climbed in the back of the limo. "Let's go to the airport."

"Yes, sir."

Dimitrios unfolded the paper. The first thing he noticed on the front page of the *Times* was a fantastic shot of three ships. At closer inspection they turned out to be a Viking longboat plus a Greek and a Roman galley moored in the bay of Thessalonica awaiting the fair. A nice-size article accompanied the photo.

He saw Ms. Hamilton's hand in the write-up. Except to give her the okay on the project, Dimitrios really hadn't been—

His thoughts were interrupted by the ring of his cell phone. He pulled it from his pocket and checked the caller ID. It was someone from the villa.

"Yassou?"

"Kalimera, Uncle. You *are* coming home today aren't you?"

His nephew sounded anxious. "I'm on my way to the airport now."

"Good. There's a lot I have to talk to you about."

"I take it things are still at an impasse with your mother."

"Yes. She refuses to discuss anything with me when she doesn't even know what I'm going to say."

"You and I have been over this before. She's afraid of losing you, Leon."

"How do I convince her that couldn't possibly happen?"

I'm not sure you can. He rubbed his eyes. "Tell you what. Tomorrow morning the three of us will sit down together and talk this out."

"Thank you. Mother's much better with you there. Can I pick you up at the airport?"

Dimitrios wasn't immune to the pleading in his nephew's voice. "It will be late. I'll have my secretary with me."

"Where's she staying?"

"I've booked her at the Mediterranean Palace."

"No problem. We'll run her by there on our way home, but it may take us a while. The traffic's horrendous. You're going to be surprised at what you see when you get here. The city's been transformed while you've been in New York.''

''I'm looking forward to viewing the finished product.''

''Besides all the booths that have gone up, the buildings and churches, even the White Tower is festooned with pennants and medieval banners. The city's been invaded with people, and there are six ships in port now.

''Wait till you get a look at the Egyptian barge from Cleopatra's time on loan for the event! Five days aren't going to be enough for people to see everything.''

''I think five days is about all our fair city will be able to handle.''

''That's what Vaso said. We had lunch with some government officials from the prime minister's office who were looking around yesterday. They said they'd never seen anything like this in their lifetime. The praise for you is pouring in already and the fair hasn't even started yet.''

''My secretary will be gratified to hear it. She's the mastermind behind the entire concept.''

''You're just saying that because you never like to take credit for anything.''

''No. If you don't believe me, I'll have Ms. Hamilton show you the contents of her portfolio after we get there.''

''I'm glad you're coming home, Uncle.''

''Me, too. See you soon.''

Dimitrios clicked off.

One look at her artwork and Leon wouldn't believe his eyes. The drawings were remarkable. When everything was over he intended to have the first sketch framed for his office.

As his private jet came into view, his cell phone went off again. "Leon? Obviously you forgot something important."

"It's Ananke."

Dimitrios should have known better than to answer that way, but his mind had been on Ms. Hamilton.

"*Yassou,* Ananke."

"It doesn't surprise me my son reached you before I did," she began without preamble. "I have to know— Is he willing to stay in school one more semester? Please tell me yes," she cried.

Her desperation found a vulnerable spot inside Dimitrios. He wasn't exactly enchanted by the bombshell his nephew had dropped on them.

"I'm still working on it."

"How soon are you coming home?"

"Late tonight. I told Leon we'd all sit down and discuss this in the morning."

"Thank you." Her voice trembled.

"Ananke? Just remember, there's only so much I can do."

"You can stop him!"

Dimitrios heaved a sigh. "If this is his destiny, then no earthly power will make a difference."

The sobbing on her end meant the conversation was over, for the time being, anyway.

He undid his seat belt. "I'll see you tomorrow," he murmured before ringing off.

As the vehicle pulled to a stop, Dimitrios levered himself from the back of the limo and hurried up the steps of the plane.

"*Kalimera, Kyrie Pandakis.*"

Instead of his pilots or his steward speaking to him in

Greek, it was Ms. Hamilton who greeted him in his native tongue as he entered the plane. It was a first for her. She never failed to surprise him.

"Kalimera," he said back to her, relieved she was here.

"Hero poli."

"It's nice to see you, too." He responded in Greek once more, impressed by this latest display of her many talents. She'd spoken with barely a trace of accent. Continuing in the same language he said, "Shall we carry on this fascinating conversation after we've fastened ourselves in?"

"I'm sorry." She reverted to English. "I didn't understand anything else you said after you told me it was nice to see me, too."

Her honesty was so refreshing, he burst out laughing. For a moment it dispelled the cloud that had enveloped him since his nephew had confided in him.

The rest of his crew welcomed him aboard, but he was barely aware of them as he gave the nod to prepare for takeoff.

"What I just said to you, Ms. Hamilton, was that I was looking forward to a lengthy discussion in Greek, but thought it would be wise to strap ourselves in first so the pilot can do his job."

"Oh." She took the seat opposite him and fastened her seat belt. "I'm afraid you've heard my full repertoire until we reach Greece. Then I'll impress you by asking where the post office is, how much does a stamp cost, that sort of thing."

His chuckle got lost in the scream of the jet engines. After a smooth liftoff it didn't take long until the plane had attained cruising speed and they could unstrap themselves.

Out of the periphery he saw that she already had her nose in the notebook she called her bible. He noticed it went everywhere with her.

"Your friend didn't mind bringing you to the airport so early?"

She lifted her head. "Yanni's on his way to Athens, so it worked out fine."

"To be with family?"

"That, and to attend the fair."

The steward chose that moment to serve them tea. Dimitrios thanked him, then sat back in his seat, wondering why her answer mattered. It was none of his business if she planned to be with her lover in Thessalonica.

As soon as the brew had cooled, he took a long swallow. It was so delicious he drank the rest without pause, then requested more.

Speaking in Greek, he complimented his steward who murmured in the same language, "She brought it on board. Insisted on steeping it herself."

Intrigued, Dimitrios flicked his gaze to his secretary. For once she had irritated him by being too absorbed with her work. "My compliments, Ms. Hamilton. This tea tastes like the proverbial nectar of the gods."

She raised her head in his direction. "According to Yanni who won't drink anything else, that's the name of it in Greek. He says it comes from the sage that grows wild on the mountains of the Peloponnese. I told him you have a sweet tooth, so he said to add honey instead of sugar. I'm glad you like it."

Dimitrios should have been appreciative of her desire to please him with a special treat. He *was* pleased. But for some reason it irritated him that Yanni had any part in her thoughtful gesture.

She opened her laptop computer. "Shall we go over the timetable of events now? I've made a hard copy for you. If there's anything you want to change, I'll enter it and print it out when we reach Greece."

In an oddly rebellious mood Dimitrios adjusted the seat so he could fully relax and close his eyes.

"Why don't you read it out loud instead. I'll interrupt if I think of something you haven't."

He sounded tired, bordering grumpy.

Alex had thought the tea might sweeten him up. Normally he was very even-tempered for a man who shouldered so much responsibility.

But she'd worked closely with him over the last six months and had started to notice a pattern to his change in mood. It only came on when he was getting ready to fly home to Greece.

If her mother was right about his past, he probably had hidden demons still to be conquered.

It happened to a lot of people. Alex's only unmarried sister chose to feel like a victim. Except for the occasional visit, she preferred to remain in California rather than come home and deal with family on a more frequent basis.

Deciding it would be best to humor her boss, Alex began reading the countdown of the first page out loud. Halfway through, she detected a change in his breathing. He was asleep.

Zeus at rest.

That's how she thought of him.

This was only the second time she'd flown in the

Pandakis jet with its eagle emblem. As on her first flight with him to San Francisco, she had the feeling she was being spirited away by the legendary Olympian god to his private kingdom in the sky.

Through her lashes, she studied his long, powerfully built body stretched out in his seat opposite her, his piercing black eyes closed for the time being.

She wished she were a painter so she could capture him on canvas. He had the bold facial structure of his Macedonian ancestors, and that beautiful olive skin born from the kiss of a hot Mediterranean sun. Yet there was something childlike in the quiet way he slept.

More handsome than the young god Adonis. The paparazzi claimed he was the lover of many women, yet faithful to none. Alex could vouch for a goodly number of females who called the office anxious to talk to him.

However, she really had no idea what he did after she left for her apartment at the end of the day. Presumably there was a certain amount of truth to the gossip in the tabloids.

But Alex regarded him in a different light. To her, raven-haired Dimitrios Pandakis could well be the supreme ruler of the gods who shaped the corporate world below. One word of displeasure from his sensuous lips was like the proverbial thunderbolt hurled at those who lied or broke oaths.

The experience nine years ago had already provided her with firsthand knowledge that he was the god of justice and mercy and a protector of the weak.

After saving her from the unwanted attentions of his cousin, he'd shown her kindness before removing the other man from her sight. But he'd taken away a lot more than that. He'd gone off with her young girl's heart.

Quite simply, his intervention changed the course of her life.

As her eyes took their fill of him, the ache to touch him intensified. More than ever she realized it would never be enough to be *just* his private secretary. Reason declared that the end of the fair would have to be the end of the road for her. The cessation of all fantasy.

Exhausted from too little sleep and her emotional struggle, she put her things away and lay back, willing oblivion to come if only for a little while.

It was a shock to finally wake up to her surroundings and discover that the interior lights had come on. Outside the plane they were cloaked in darkness.

She checked her watch. Heavens. How could she have been asleep seven hours?

Though alone for the moment, she was conscious of the sound of male voices coming from the cockpit area. Judging by their chuckles, someone was telling an amusing tale.

Probably she'd snored, or her stomach had growled so loudly they'd all heard it. Either possibility was so humiliating, Alex shot out of her seat and used the time to freshen up in the bathroom.

While she was repinning her hair to secure it better after her long sleep, she noted that the plane had started to encounter some turbulence. She didn't pay much attention to it until the Fasten Seat Belts sign flashed overhead.

Alex put in the last pin, then left the bathroom and hurried to her seat. As she strapped herself in, she saw Dimitrios emerge from the cockpit, his expression sober.

"I was about to do that for—"

But she wasn't destined to hear him say anything else

because the plane hit an air pocket, sending him flying. He crashed against the wall. By the position of his body, he'd been knocked unconscious. She saw blood.

"*Dimitrios!*"

They were dropping out of the sky as if being pulled toward a giant lodestone.

Please, God. Don't let anything happen to him.

CHAPTER THREE

"HE'S coming around."

"Don't let him move his head."

"No. I've got him."

"An AirMed helicopter will meet us when we land."

"The bleeding's stopped."

"That's good. Keep that compress over the wound."

"Do you think his arm is broken?"

"No. Nothing's broken that I see, but he's going to have an ugly bruise on his shoulder for a while."

Dimitrios had been hearing voices for the last few minutes. Now he was aware of stinging at the crown of his head. Slowly his body was coming back to life.

Mingled with the smell of alcohol was a delicious scent, like pears, that permeated his nostrils. It came from a smooth, cool hand cupping his jaw along the side of his face. He seemed to be resting on something soft and warm. His eyelids fluttered open.

Waves of dizziness assailed him. He blinked several times until his gaze focused on a pair of soulful green eyes staring down at him. They seemed to take up her whole face.

Good Lord. What were they both doing on the floor of the plane with his head in her lap?

"Ms. Hamilton?"

"Thank heaven you know me," she whispered emotionally.

"Welcome back," came the voice of his copilot. Both

he and the steward had to be standing somewhere near his feet.

Dimitrios blinked again. Maybe it was the angle of the recessed lighting that made him think moisture clung to his secretary's long, silky lashes. He'd never seen her without her steel-rimmed glasses. She had flawless skin and a beautifully shaped mouth.

"What happened?"

"We hit an air pocket before you could make it to your seat," she explained.

"I remember now," he muttered on a groan. "How soon before we land?"

His copilot hunkered at his side. "We're approaching Macedonia International now."

Dimitrios started to get up, but all three of them held him down. "Don't move," his steward ordered. "You have a lump on the top of your head and must be seen by a doctor."

"I heard you say nothing was broken. Let me up," he ordered.

Still they restrained him. *Damnation.*

He felt the tightening of his secretary's diaphragm before she asked, "How many stones are there in my ring?"

What?

She held the top of her hand in front of his eyes so he couldn't possibly miss it.

"Five."

"Good. There's nothing wrong with his vision, gentlemen. I think Kyrie Pandakis is recovered enough to get to his seat."

His steward shook his head. "I don't know—"

"Well I *do!* Don't worry. I'll take full responsibility

if anything should happen to him. Now if you'll both assist me and we're all very careful, we can get him strapped in before we begin our descent.

"Don't you dare pass out on me now," her lips whispered against his ear before she told the two men to support his elbows so he could stand up.

Dimitrios could count on the fingers of one hand the times in his life when he'd been filled with wonder. To see his steward and copilot cowed into submission without further remonstration qualified as one of them. Once helped into his seat and buckled in, he gripped the arm rests, fighting not to succumb to his dizziness and fall over again.

His head felt like it weighed a thousand pounds. In fact it hurt like hell except for that moment when her lips brushed his ear. Then all he could feel was a little explosion of electricity shooting through his system.

"You see?" He heard her speak to his staff from her seat. "He's fine. Tell the pilot to cancel the helicopter. If Kyrie Pandakis isn't well after he gets home, his family will send for his doctor."

After more hesitation, his copilot went to the cockpit to do her bidding. The steward remained nearby, still looking unsure about things. It had to be a first for him.

"Is this your wish?" he demanded

"As my secretary said, I'm all right. Thank you for your help and concern. Tell the pilot everyone is grateful he was able to stabilize the plane in time."

The other man gave a reluctant nod before disappearing.

"When the world stops spinning, Ms. Hamilton, remind me to give you a bonus for keeping a cool head. It must have been a terrifying experience for you."

"Only when I saw you go flying."

The Fasten Seat Belts sign went on. They were beginning their descent. His head swam.

"It won't be long now." Her voice seemed to come from a long way off.

The next thing he was aware of was his secretary bending over him to undo his seat belt. He could smell the pear scent once more.

"We're home, Mr. Pandakis."

"What happened to Kyrie?"

She ignored his question. "Stand up and lean against me while we exit the plane."

His dizziness was as bad on the ground as in the air. He put his arm around her shoulders and they started for the door. A few steps from the entrance he had to cling to her.

Who would have guessed at the warm, full curves and flare of womanly hips hidden beneath the folds of the shapeless, loose-fitting outfit she wore.

Why in heaven's name did she dress in clothes that masked such a voluptuous figure? For that matter, why didn't she wear contacts? Her steel-rimmed glasses hid one of her best assets. It didn't make any sense.

"Come on," she urged. "We're almost there."

"Give me another minute." The world was still whirling. So were his senses. This sharp awareness of her as a flesh-and-blood woman had caught him completely by surprise.

The steward opened the door.

Dimitrios heard footsteps on the stairs leading up to the plane's entrance. "Uncle?"

When a dark-haired man close to Alex's age suddenly appeared in the opening, she didn't know who looked more surprised. Somehow she'd thought his nephew would be younger.

He halted mid-stride when he saw his uncle clinging to her. Dimitrios had closed his eyes for a moment. Given his pallor, she could understand why his nephew had concern written all over his face.

"Kyrie Pandakis has had a slight accident. He's a little dizzy from a bump on the head, but it's nothing serious," she assured him. "If you'd like to help your uncle out to the car, I'll gather my things and be right with you."

"Of course." He rushed forward and put his arm around his uncle. "Do you think you can make it now, Uncle?" The deep affection in his voice touched Alex.

"As soon as I introduce the two of you," came the dry response. "Leon? This is my secretary, the legendary Ms. Hamilton." He was weaving on his feet as he said it.

She eyed his nephew, hoping he received her silent message. "We'll have time for that later. Right now what's important is to get you home."

Between Leon and the two pilots, Dimitrios was helped to the car with little problem. Alex followed with her purse and briefcase. The steward stowed it in the trunk with her suitcase, then helped her into the front passenger seat.

Dimitrios had been put in back so he could spread out. She winced at the shadows beneath his eyes. He would never admit to the horrendous pain he was in.

She thanked the staff, then told Leon to step on it. He obviously didn't need any urging because the car accelerated at a faster speed than she imagined was allowed.

"How long will it take to reach the Mediterranean

Palace?'' She asked this in a low tone as they drove away from the plane.

"Normally fifteen minutes," he whispered, "but because of the tourists in town for the fair, the traffic is heavy at all hours now. It could take longer."

"Ms. Hamilton won't be staying at the hotel, Leon. Drive us straight to the villa."

Alex caught the surprised glance Leon flashed his uncle over his shoulder. But she understood. Dimitrios felt too ill to put up with any detours tonight.

She leaned closer to his nephew. Mouthing the words, she said, "As soon as we get him home, I'll take a taxi to the hotel."

He nodded.

With that understood, she moved next to the door so she could rest her head against the glass.

It was hard to believe she was in Greece.

She should be thrilled, exhilarated. It was a lovely warm night. They were driving through one of the oldest cities in Europe. Some sites dated back to 2300 B.C. She was passing over ground of saints and scholars.

There was so much history to absorb. But after the shock she'd lived through, she was too enervated to do anything more than close her eyes.

Only one thing mattered. Dimitrios was alive and seemingly in one piece. His injuries could have been so much worse. She still hadn't recovered from seeing his big body hurtled to the floor of the plane, lifeless.

If Alex needed proof of what he meant to her, that experience would stand out for all time as the defining moment.

At one point she'd seen Leon pull out his cell phone and make several calls. Therefore it didn't surprise her that the guard at the gate of the estate let them through without Leon having to brake.

A sizable group of people were assembled in the courtyard by the time they wound around the tree-lined drive to the front of the ochre-toned villa. Large and square-shaped in design, it looked fairly impregnable and quite unlike what Alex had imagined.

That was probably because she was used to seeing travel brochures with pictures of the white, cube-style villas nestled close together on the Greek Islands.

Two women rushed forward. One old, with a face that looked a trifle wizened from being in the sun too long. The other fortyish and attractive, with big brown eyes that reminded Alex of Leon.

"Dimitrios!" they both cried at once as his nephew got out of the car and opened the back door for him. A spate of Greek Alex couldn't understand poured out of both women. One of the male staff members somebody called Kristofor worked with Leon to help his uncle from the car.

The rest of the staff stood by with anxious expressions. It was evident that everyone held Kyrie Pandakis in great affection and were upset to see him incapacitated in any way.

Alex knew just how they felt.

Relieved he was home in the comfort of his family, she climbed out of the front seat to get her things from the trunk. To her surprise she caught the full brunt of headlights from a taxi that had pulled up behind the car. It had gotten here quickly.

More conversation in Greek ensued. This time it was Dimitrios's voice overriding everyone else's. A subdued, confused-looking Leon walked to the taxi. Alex saw him pull some money from his wallet and pay the driver, who backed around and took off.

"Everyone speak English, please," Dimitrios declared. For a man who was barely hanging on, his voice sounded amazingly strong and authoritative.

"My secretary, Ms. Hamilton, will be our houseguest for a while. Serilda? If you will be kind enough to prepare the guest room down the hall from mine for her. Nicholas? Please bring her things from the back of the car."

The staff seemed to take everything as a matter of course, but Alex didn't dare make a scene right then. Not in front of the woman who had to be Leon's mother, Ananke. She stared at Alex like she was a visitor from another planet.

When they entered the palatial villa, it felt like Alex had just stepped into another time period. The flavor of old Byzantium called out to her. Under other circumstances she would love to explore every inch of it, learn the story behind every exquisite artifact.

But Alex could hear her mother's warning. *Go to Greece, do your job, don't go near his family, then come straight home.*

The front door clicked shut behind her. She had no choice but to follow Dimitrios who, with help, managed to make it down two hallways to his own suite of rooms.

Though the lump on his head was hidden, Alex could see that some of his black hair was still matted with blood, a potent reminder of an experience that could have taken his life.

At the thought, she felt sickness sweep over her. Her steps slowed until the moment of sudden weakness passed.

Leon's mother stayed right with him, talking in Greek to her son even though Dimitrios had requested otherwise.

"Ms. Hamilton?" he called over his shoulder without looking at her. "When you've freshened up, please come to my bedroom. There's some business we have to discuss."

"I'll come now if you'd like." The sooner he said what he had to say, the sooner she'd be able to phone for another taxi and slip away. Thanks to Yanni, she could do that much for herself in Greek without anyone's help.

"I'd like," she heard him mutter.

His suite came as a complete surprise. It was modern and unquestionably masculine down to the tan and black striped bedspread. Alex sank down on one of two chairs arranged around a coffee table while Leon and Kristofor helped Dimitrios stretch out on top of the bed.

His eyes were closed. He looked wan and exhausted. There was blood on his rumpled shirt, which was partway unbuttoned, revealing a dusting of black hair on his chest. Alex closed her eyes to shut out the sight before her.

She'd never loved him more. All she wanted to do was crawl onto the king-size bed and take care of him. Hold him like she'd done on the plane. Her arms ached from the loss.

While she'd steadied his head, she'd been able to study the tiny lines that radiated from around his eyes, the set of his jaw, the sensuality of his male mouth she yearned to cover with her own.

"Serilda has called for the doctor. Until he has examined you, you're not to discuss business or anything else.''

''Mother's right, Uncle. Let me help you get ready for bed.''

''As you can both see, I'm fine, just dizzy. It will pass. I appreciate your concern, but right now Ms. Hamilton and I have matters to discuss that won't wait.''

''I'm sure she's exhausted, too,'' Ananke persisted.

Sensing Dimitrios's impatience simmering beneath the surface Alex said, ''Actually I slept seven hours on the plane and feel very well rested. I promise I won't work your brother-in-law too long.''

''Leon? Will you bring Ms. Hamilton's briefcase to her?''

His nephew nodded before hurrying out of the room.

Alex watched the other woman's hands curl into fists at her side. ''I'll bring you some tea and pain killers.''

''I—I don't think he should have anything yet.''

At Alex's interjection, Ananke flashed her a hostile glance.

''I only mentioned it, Mrs. Pandakis, because I'm sure he has suffered a concussion.''

Despite his injury Dimitrios seemed to be alert enough to address his sister-in-law. ''Ask the cook to make tea and sandwiches, Ananke. My secretary slept through lunch and dinner and must be starving by now.''

Her brown eyes glittered angrily before she left the room.

''Here's your briefcase, Ms. Hamilton.''

''Thank you.''

''Leon— I'm glad you came to the plane. I couldn't have gotten along without your help. In the morning, we'll have that talk. All right?''

"Only if you're feeling much better, Uncle."

"I'm sure I will. Would you mind closing the door on your way out?"

"No. Of course not." His brown gaze darted to Alex. "Good night, Ms. Hamilton."

"Good night. It was very nice to meet you."

A strange silence filled the room after he'd gone.

Alex was relieved to see Dimitrios's eyes had closed. Finally he could rest. That's why it came as a surprise when he spoke to her.

"After today's experience, I realize that along with your many attributes, you were born with an ability to read minds, too."

"You mean about my canceling the helicopter."

"Among other things."

"I did it for self-preservation."

"How so?"

"You're Thessalonica's favorite son. The media would've had a field day if word had leaked out that you were being transported to the hospital from the plane. I'd have been forced to ward them off. To be honest, I didn't particularly relish the thought after—"

"After you thought it was the end, and your life flashed before your eyes?"

She bowed her head. "Something like that, yes." Except that was a lie. There'd only been one thought on her mind. *One* man.

"I was concerned about the publicity. It would probably have given your government officials a heart attack to know you were hurt this close to the trade fair. As it is, your name's going to be all over the news by morning."

"You think?" came the deep voice.

It amazed her he had the energy to tease in his condition.

"I'm sure your loyal pilot was shaken by the incident. No doubt he issued some strict orders to the hospital to stand by because they were going to be receiving some very precious cargo.

"Right now the phones are probably ringing off the hook to every journalist that you're back in Greece and something terrible happened to you in flight."

"Something did."

His comment sounded faintly cryptic. She kneaded her hands together.

"We don't have any business to discuss tonight. Why did you ask me to come in here?"

"You're the mind reader, Ms. Hamilton. You tell me."

She took a steadying breath. "I think your sister-in-law was right. You need rest, and I need to call the hotel."

"Don't worry about canceling the reservation. I'll take care of it."

"That's the problem. You *mustn't* do that."

His eyes opened. He seemed very alert all of a sudden.

"Why not? If I'm to be confined over the next few days, it makes the most sense."

"The hotel is simply a place to sleep." She tried reasoning with him. "I'll be available to you at all hours otherwise."

The tension was mounting. "What aren't you telling me?"

She'd seen him in this mood before. He wouldn't give up until he had the answer he wanted. She'd learned from past experience it was pointless to try to thwart him.

"Someone else is staying with me."

His black eyes penetrated the distance between them. "Yanni?" he asked in a deceptively silken voice.

"No. His name is Michael. I don't think I've mentioned him before."

"No, I don't believe you have. Does this Michael appreciate the fact that you're here on business?"

"Yes. Of course. Please don't think that I was attempting to take advantage of your generosity. I'm willing to pay for the room personally." She didn't believe it was necessary to mention Michael's friends.

"Do you suppose he'll live if I ask you to stay here at the villa until I'm back to normal?"

Unless his pain was much worse, she couldn't understand why he sounded so surly. Under normal circumstances he never allowed any weakness to show.

Obviously the trade fair was even more important to him than he'd let on. It was only natural he didn't want anything to go wrong this close to the opening. The thing to do was placate him until he started feeling better and could walk around without too much discomfort.

When she thought about it, she realized he was used to having her in calling distance at the office. Oftentimes they sat across from each other at his desk to do business until late. She could see it would frustrate him to have to phone back and forth to the hotel.

"Apparently my request is causing you grief."

At the sarcastic comment, heat filled her cheeks. "Not at all!" she rushed to assure him. "I was just thinking that I have to get something from him."

"Leon can run by the hotel in the morning and pick up whatever it is you need, unless you require it tonight."

"Oh, no. I— It's a costume."

A half-smile broke the corner of his mouth. For some reason her comment had pleased him.

"Let me guess. For your television interview you're going to appear as Thessalonica, wife of the King of Macedonia."

She chuckled softly. "It's not for me. In any case I won't be going anywhere near the media."

"Who then?"

"The man in charge."

"If you're referring to me, I haven't been in charge of anything since you took over Mrs. Landau's job."

Not to be put off, she said, "You'll need to try it on first to make certain it fits properly before you appear on camera."

He stirred as if he were trying to get up, but then he slumped back. It revealed so much.

"You actually went to the trouble to find a costume for me?"

She swallowed hard. "I had it made."

After a pregnant silence, "Give me a clue."

"Well—you were a military commander of Thessalonica in the early fourth century."

"There were dozens of those." His voice grated.

"This one was appointed by the Emperor Maximian to take his place."

"As I recall, Maximian persecuted Christians."

"That's right, but this commander was a defender of Christ. For defying the emperor he was cast into prison. Then an angel of God came to him and told him to be brave. A few days later he was martyred and became a saint."

Another silence ensued. Much longer this time. He'd guessed who it was.

Before she could hear him say it, there was a rap on the door. Then the housekeeper appeared with a tray. Behind her came Ananke and Leon, followed by a bearded, middle-aged man carrying a doctor's bag.

"So, Dimitrios. I hear you received a big bump on your head. Let me take a look at it."

Alex stood up to leave.

"Sit down and eat, Ms. Hamilton," Dimitrios ordered her.

The doctor winked at her. "Dimitrios never did make a good patient. Since he has spoken, you'd better obey."

The housekeeper set the tray down on the table, then left while the other two stood waiting to hear what the doctor had to say. Alex had little choice but to abide by her boss's wishes.

After checking Dimitrios's vital signs, the doctor asked Leon to bring him some warm water from the bathroom. He explained he was going to clean the wound.

As he examined it he said, "Tell me how this happened."

"Ms. Hamilton knows more about it than I do," came the wry response.

Everyone looked at Alex, who had to finish swallowing her bite of sandwich before she could say anything.

"As he was coming back to his seat, the plane hit an air pocket. His body flew, and his head hit the wall of the plane knocking him unconscious." It was still distressing to recall the incident, let alone talk about it.

"Hmm. Considering what you've been through, Dimitrios, you seem in amazingly good shape. But I don't doubt you've got a concussion.

"I'm not going to give you anything for the pain yet. Someone will have to watch you for the next twelve hours. If you become ill or sleep too long, then you'll have to be brought to my office for an X ray.

"However, if all goes well, and I think it will, by noon tomorrow you can start to eat and drink what sounds good to you. You'll be dizzy for a time. Don't try to overdo when you first get up. Call me if you have any questions."

He closed his doctor bag and started to leave. Ananke accompanied him to the door. "I'll stay with him."

"I'll trade off with you, Mother."

"I appreciate both your offers, but Ms. Hamilton has already agreed to sit up with me."

His declaration shocked everyone, especially Alex, who almost fell off the chair at the lie.

"She slept most of the way over on the plane," he continued. "Now that she's awake and I'm too dizzy to go sleep, we'll be able to get our work done without interruption."

"But you can't expect your secretary—"

"My secretary has the entire responsibility of the trade fair on her shoulders, Ananke," he cut in. "She needs tonight to go over the details with me. If I should suddenly lose consciousness, she's perfectly capable of letting you know. Isn't that true, Ms. Hamilton?"

The tension in the room was unbearable. There were strange undercurrents Alex couldn't begin to understand. His nephew looked confused and hurt. Along with an angry look at Alex, his sister-in-law reflected her son's feelings. Unfortunately Dimitrios was waiting for an answer.

"Yes, of course."

CHAPTER FOUR

ALEX felt tremendous guilt to hear the bedroom door close behind Leon and Ananke.

"Don't worry, they're going to be fine," Dimitrios murmured. "There are things I know that you don't. Tonight I'm not up to anything but a little peace and quiet. With you here to be my own guardian angel, I'll be assured of the rest I crave."

One glance at the lines of strain around his nose and mouth and she could tell his energy was spent. No doubt at this point he was starting to feel other aches and pains.

She slid out of the chair and turned off all the lights, hoping it would help. The sigh that escaped his throat told her she'd done the right thing. Taking advantage of the dark, she removed her glasses and put them on the table.

"This is almost as cozy as the plane. I don't suppose you'd come over here and hold my head again."

Alex was surprised by his banter, but she knew how awful it was to be dizzy. Combined with unrelieved pain, he had to be in a terrible state. She wished she could do what her mother did when her father suffered from a severe migraine.

If Alex had the temerity, she would sit next to him and use the tips of her fingers to tickle his face until he fell asleep. First his forehead, then across his brows and eyelids, down his straight nose to his mouth.

Though it was dark, it wasn't pitch black by any

means. Alex was able to use her eyes for fingers. She imagined tracing a line over every masculine feature and plane of a face that was so beautiful to her.

An hour must have passed before she saw the drawn look around his mouth relax. He was finally asleep. She found a light blanket and put it over him.

For the rest of the night she kept a constant vigil. Every so often she checked his pulse and felt to see if he was running a temperature.

Fearful he might go into too deep a sleep, she listened carefully for any change of sound in his breathing. At one point the urge to touch him was so strong, she smoothed the black curls off his forehead before sitting in the chair she'd pulled next to him. The joy of taking care of him was inexplicable.

At five to ten, the sun spread spokes of light across the bed through the shutters. As she leaned over once more to check his pulse, his eyelids opened.

He caught her hand with surprising strength before she could remove it. Though she hadn't escaped in time for him to realize what she'd been doing, it proved he'd passed through the period of crisis without problem.

His black eyes glanced at the chair, then seemed to look straight into her soul. "You sat next to me all night?"

"Yes." Fearful he'd get the wrong idea she said, "I told you before you went to sleep, you're the most important person in Thessalonica. If anything had gone wrong during the night, I wanted to be prepared to handle it in case your doctor needed to be phoned. We couldn't afford for the media to know anything."

As an afterthought she blurted, "Fortunately this

morning your pupils don't look dilated, so I'm assuming you're feeling better.''

"I'm still a little dizzy, but I only see one pair of green eyes this morning instead of three.''

Alex trembled that he'd even noticed her eyes, but she didn't dare take it personally.

"That's a very good sign you're on your way to a full recovery.'' Hard as it was to separate herself from him, she moved the chair to the table. "Your family's going to be delighted with the news.''

"Unfortunately I'm not delighted to see how exhausted you are,'' came the less than flattering remark, underlining her belief that his comment about her eyes held no significance whatsoever.

"I catnapped here and there. Do you feel ready for something to eat or drink?''

"Like you, I'm ravenous, and could swallow a gallon of that sage tea with honey.'' He sounded like he meant it.

"Let me find your housekee—''

"You're going to bed!'' he interrupted her. "I'll ring the kitchen and ask them to send us trays. They'll deliver one to your room. Then I want you to sleep for as long as you need to. We'll talk business later in the day when you're up and feeling refreshed.''

She was his secretary and had been banished to the guest bedroom. It was the surest sign that he was once more in command.

Without further words passing between them, she left his room and shut the door. At the click, she felt a death knell in her heart because those precious moments of intimacy while he'd been at his most vulnerable would never come her way again.

A few minutes later she stood beneath a hot shower, attempting to shut out her mother's warning. But it was too late.

I'm afraid for you to go to Greece. It can only put you on a more intimate footing with him without getting anything back in return.

Dimitrios moved slowly to reach for the phone. His housekeeper sounded relieved he was well enough to eat. He told her to send one breakfast tray to the guest room and another to his bedroom.

After he hung up, he realized Ms. Hamilton must have covered him with a blanket during the night.

She'd done more than that. He'd felt her fingers like little angel wings brushing his forehead. Though it was hours since the experience, he could still feel her touch. So soft...yet it had electrified him. He'd actually wanted to pull her down on the bed next to him and...

Lord. The accident on the plane must have done something more serious to him than he'd thought. Never in all these years had he been tempted to break his vow and take a woman to bed.

Frustrated and shocked by feelings of desire for his secretary, of all women, he made another vow that he wouldn't allow her to disturb him again.

Carefully pushing the blanket aside, he got off the bed. The action reminded him he'd hurt his shoulder. He winced while he clung to the nightstand, waiting for his equilibrium to return.

Every muscle in his body ached, but at least he was standing on his own. It didn't surprise him to hear a knock on the door. Everyone else would have been up for several hours.

"Uncle? Serilda said you called for breakfast. Can I come in?"

"Of course."

His nephew rushed over the threshold. He looked worried to see Dimitrios standing by the bed. "Should you be up yet?"

"I'm all right."

"That's a great relief. Let me help you into the shower."

"Tell you what. Stay close by while I try to make it on my own."

It was a struggle, but he managed without having to rely on his nephew for support.

"Be careful, Uncle. The doctor said not to get your head wet for another day."

"Thank you for the reminder."

The hot spray felt good on his sore shoulder. Deciding to forgo a shave, he dressed in a clean robe. By the time he'd joined his nephew for breakfast, he was feeling reasonably normal except for certain memory flashes. He could still remember being held in her arms on the plane, of being touched when she'd thought him asleep.

"I hope Ms. Hamilton didn't allow you to stay up too late."

Dimitrios finished off his orange juice in one swallow. When he put the empty glass down he said, "You don't have to worry. She's that rare secretary who anticipates my every need." It would be too much to hope she would repeat last night's experience tonight.

Once again it dawned on Dimitrios he was entertaining thoughts that had no place being there. He groaned at his lack of mental discipline. Damn if the room didn't spin when he moved his head too fast.

"I'm glad you're so much better, Uncle."

That was debatable. But a few minutes later, after he'd consumed a cheese omelette and butter biscuits, he felt ready to take care of a little personal business.

"I might have an errand for you to run. Afterward, we'll go out on the terrace with your mother and talk. Would you mind handing me my cell phone? It's in my suit jacket hanging on the chair. I'll also need the phone directory."

"Don't move. I'll get everything."

Once his nephew gave him both items, he looked up the number of the hotel and called reception.

"Mediterranean Palace. *Kalimera.*"

"*Kalimera.* This is Dimitrios Pandakis. Put me through to Ms. Hamilton's suite, please. It's booked in my name."

"Mr. Pandakis! We heard you'd had an accident."

"A small one, but I'm fine."

"I'm pleased to hear it. Just a moment and I'll put you through."

"Thank you."

On the third ring, a man speaking English answered the phone. "Better late than never, Alexandra, darling. What happened? I was beginning to wonder if Zeus had whisked you off to parts unknown in that private jet of his, never to be seen again."

Dimitrios felt a negative rush of adrenaline. "This is Dimitrios Pandakis. Sorry to disappoint you. Ms. Hamilton is staying at my villa for the moment. This *is* Michael, I presume."

"That's right."

"My secretary's asleep, but I'm sure she'll be in touch

with you as soon as she wakens. She mentioned a costume. Do you have it with you?''

''Yes.''

''I'll be sending my nephew for it within the half hour. His name is Leon Pandakis.''

''If you'll tell your nephew to meet me at the front desk, I'll wait there for him.''

''How will he know you?''

''I'll be carrying a golden scepter in one hand.''

He clutched his phone tighter. *She'd really had a costume of Saint Dimitrios made for him?*

''Thank you, Michael.''

''You're welcome, Mr. Pandakis.''

After the line went dead he felt the childish urge to knock the man's block off. What the heck was wrong with him?

''Uncle? Are you all right? Are you nauseous?''

He eyed Leon, unable to explain to himself, let alone his nephew, the unsettling mixture of emotions running through him.

''No. Do me a favor and run by the Mediterranean Palace. There'll be a man who's a friend of Ms. Hamilton's waiting in the lobby. He'll be carrying a costume. You'll recognize him because he'll be holding a gold scepter.''

''That sounds interesting. I'll go right away.''

''Thank you, Leon. On your way out will you ask one of the maids to bring me the morning paper?''

He nodded. ''Promise me you won't move while I'm gone.''

''You have my word.''

As soon as his nephew left, he phoned Stavros, who sounded touchingly emotional to hear that Dimitrios was on the mend after his accident. Apparently the whole family had heard about the plane mishap over the morning news and were worried about him.

Dimitrios rushed to assure him he was fine. During the course of their conversation, Serilda brought him the newspaper, then slipped out of the bedroom with his empty tray.

It was just as his secretary had predicted. The pilot's call to the hospital had made front-page headlines. Damn the media.

He tossed the paper aside in disgust. In a foul mood, he told Stavros he'd call him later. After they hung up, he knew he ought to ring Vaso, at least, but he couldn't bring himself to do it.

The way the man named Michael had answered the phone—"Alexandra, darling"—not even waiting to find out if she was the person calling had set his teeth on edge.

Dimitrios couldn't help but wonder how soon Yanni would show up in Thessalonica. Where and when was Ms. Hamilton planning to meet *him*?

His secretary was going to be stretched pretty thin to accommodate both men and do her job at the same time.

Though she'd never done anything to disappoint him or make him angry, it pleased him to know she was in the guest bedroom sleeping alone for a change. He wagered neither man would be happy to learn she'd spent last night with him.

Would she tell either of them the exact nature of her ministrations, and why? Or was she a tease? He supposed it was possible his perfect secretary was as deceitful as the next woman when it came to a man. It would be well to keep that in mind.

"I'm back!"

His nephew entered the room for the second time that morning carrying a garment bag over one arm and a golden scepter in the other. He laid everything on the unmade bed.

"I see you found Michael."

"He was impossible to miss. I think he was a little worried because this was supposed to be a surprise for you."

"My secretary already told me about it."

"I don't think he realized that. He was nice. So American, you know? But really funny."

Dimitrios could have done without Leon's favorable observations. On the other hand, he had no right to criticize anything. After all, he'd sent his nephew on that errand for the specific purpose of learning more about the man Ms. Hamilton would be sharing a room with while she was in Greece.

If his curiosity over his secretary didn't stop, Dimitrios was going to be in deep trouble.

"Do you know what it is, Uncle?"

The question brought him back from plaguing thoughts. "I have a fairly good idea."

"Shall I unzip the bag for you?"

"Under the circumstances, I think I'll let my secretary do the honors when she wakes up."

"Is it for you?"

"I'm afraid so."

His nephew grinned. "She certainly doesn't know you very well if she thinks she can get you to wear a costume to the fair."

You'd be shocked if you knew how well she reads my

mind, Leon. That's the problem. That's why she's managed to get under my skin without my realizing it.

"It's the thought that counts," Dimitrios muttered. "I presume your mother is up."

"Hours ago."

"Then let's find her. On our way out, would you mind hanging the costume in my closet?"

"I'll do it right now."

It couldn't be six in the evening! But it was.

Anxious to find out how her host was feeling, Alex sprang from the bed, incredulous that she'd slept so long again. Her body clock was completely off kilter.

Luckily she'd had a shower before going to bed. Once she was dressed in one of her matronly suits, it was her hair that took time to fix. While she stood in front of the bathroom mirror, she remembered leaving her glasses in his bedroom.

Alarmed because anyone looking through the lenses would know they were clear glass, she realized how vital it was to get them back as soon as possible. It would provide her with a good excuse to check up on Dimitrios at the same time. But before she did anything else, she needed to make a couple of important phone calls.

To her chagrin, Michael and his friends weren't in the hotel room. She left a message welcoming them to Thessalonica. After explaining that she'd have to stay at the villa another night because her boss had met with a minor accident, she assured Michael she'd be in touch tomorrow morning.

With that done, she phoned her parents, who were greatly relieved to know she was all right. Word of the plane mishap that had injured Mr. Pandakis had even made the news in Paterson.

She didn't let on that she hadn't spent the first night at her hotel. Though she knew her mom would understand if told about the unusual circumstances, it would still worry her. It was better to say nothing until she could leave the villa.

She hung up with the promise that she'd phone them sometime tomorrow. She hoped by then she'd be at the hotel.

With the calls out of the way, she left the guest room and went down the hall to his suite. She knocked, wondering if he was inside.

"The door's open."

Hearing his deep voice made her heart leap. She pushed on it and entered.

He was sitting on top of his bed with his back against the headboard, listening to the news coming from the television. Her gaze traveled from his sandaled feet to the white sailor pants and royal blue knit shirt. The kind with the short sleeves and ribbing that looked good only on a man with some muscle.

She swallowed hard because Dimitrios's arms were darkly tanned and as powerful looking as his legs. If she could paint him like this she'd entitle it, Zeus Reflecting.

Embarrassed to be caught staring, she reached for her glasses, which were still sitting on the coffee table.

He'd improved a great deal since morning. His color had returned. She was pleased to see that the bruised look beneath his eyes had almost disappeared. It made her wonder at her temerity in touching him as she'd done last night.

With a flick of the remote, he turned off the television

and studied her. "You look rested, Ms. Hamilton. Come all the way in. Dinner will be here before long. In the meantime, we have work to do."

She reached for her briefcase and walked over to the coffee table. "You must be feeling better."

"I'm getting there. You said you'd made a copy for me of the countdown of events."

"Yes. But should you use your eyes yet? Reading might be bad for your headache."

"I've read the morning and evening papers from cover to cover and feel none the worse for it."

He sounded out of sorts. Some people didn't have as hard a time as others staying down while they were convalescing. Dimitrios was one of those others. Her boss was about as happy as a restless panther trapped inside a cage, going around and around the bars looking for a way to escape.

She dove into her briefcase and found the wanted item. "Here you are." After putting it on the bed next to him, she pulled out her laptop.

Once she'd set the computer on her thighs and turned it on, she brought up the file in question. "If you want to start, I'm ready to make any changes."

"Bring your chair closer so we don't have to shout at each other."

Alex wasn't aware they'd been shouting. In fact he'd just spoken to her in a low voice, and she'd been able to hear him perfectly. But she did as he suggested.

Lifting her head in anticipation of what he would ask to be added or deleted, her attention was caught by the sight of a gold scepter lying across the quilt next to the footboard of the bed. She hadn't noticed it when she'd entered his bedroom.

Her questioning gaze darted to her boss. He, in turn, eyed her with a complacent expression that didn't fool her.

"I found I wanted to see it," he confessed, "so I sent Leon to the hotel this morning. Michael met him in the lobby with it."

Uh, oh.

Had Dimitrios learned there were two actors staying there, as well? Not that he would have cared. It was just that she hadn't mentioned the others, and she didn't want any unnecessary talk to go on.

"Your doctor wasn't kidding when he said you made a terrible patient. If I'd known you were going to be so bored today, I would have asked Stavros to come over and keep you company."

Still worked, up she added, "Something tells me you were the kind of little boy who sneaked a look at your Christmas presents long before it was time to open them."

"Guilty on all counts."

Alex took a deep breath, willing herself to calm down. "What do you think of it?"

"I haven't seen it yet. Leon hung the garment bag in my closet. I thought I'd wait until you unveiled it before my eyes."

"Considering you went to such lengths to get it, I'm puzzled you would show that much forbearance."

"Some surprises are worth savoring."

She was stunned that he would have bothered with any of it.

"To be honest, I haven't seen it myself. I gave the seamstress a sketch months ago. It wasn't ready until the last second, so Michael picked it up for me."

"Why don't we have a sneak preview before dinner."

"I thought you wanted to work."

"Indirectly, I would say a costume to promote publicity for the fair falls under that particular umbrella."

Her hands tightened on her laptop before she got up and put it on the coffee table.

Certain things in life were private. If she were his fiancée or his wife, she couldn't imagine anything more wonderful than having the right to be in his bedroom, rummaging around in his walk-in closet, handling his clothes.

This was the danger her mother had talked about. To share all this with him—*except the most important thing*.

"What color is the bag?" she called to him.

"Dark blue."

He had a good size wardrobe, and she saw several bags matching that description. Before looking inside each one, she decided to open the floor-length cupboard. Maybe Leon had hung it in there so it would be easier to find again.

What she discovered caused her to forget why she was in there. Both sections contained boxes full of trophies, plaques and cups lying in haphazard fashion, some large, some small. Dozens of them.

One thing was clear from some of the trophies depicting a man in climbing gear with a pickax. He was an expert mountaineer.

Most of the engravings were in foreign languages, including Greek, but a few were in English. He'd climbed all over the world. There were dates going back fifteen years, yet there was one as recent as this year.

She remembered a trip he'd taken in June. He said he'd be out of the office a week and she wouldn't be able to reach him unless he phoned her. If there was a problem, she should consult Stavros.

He'd returned with a deep tan. Alex had assumed he'd gone sailing on the Aegean or some such thing. She had no idea the mountains were his great love.

"You haven't lost your way in there, have you, Ms. Hamilton?"

She shut the cupboard abruptly. "I'll be right out."

Without wasting any more time, she felt the bags until she found one that she could tell didn't contain a man's suit jacket.

Emerging from the closet, she walked over to her chair and unzipped it. A soft gasp escaped her throat when she held it up and saw what a fabulous job the seamstress had done.

Faithful to the colored sketch Alex had made from the well-known Greek icon depicting Saint Dimitrios on his horse, the short-sleeved, hip-length vest was authentic in every detail.

She found a pair of dark gold braided boot covers in the bottom of the bag. They were meant to hide his shoes and hug the trousers to his legs at a point above the calves.

Along with the boots, Cossack-style rust trousers and a great flowing ruby cape completed the outfit.

"Bring everything closer."

She did his bidding. "You have to visualize yourself on horseback wearing all this and carrying your scepter, of course." He would look magnificent.

One black eyebrow lifted. "Did you arrange for a mount, too? Am I to be interviewed on the back of it?"

No amount of self-control could hide the blush that swept up her neck and face.

On cue a knock sounded at the door causing Alex's head to swerve around.

"Uncle? I've brought your dinner." The next thing she knew Leon came into the room wheeling a tea cart laden with food. "I hope you're hungry because the cook outdid—"

He paused mid-sentence when he saw her standing next to the bed holding up the costume.

"I'm sorry. I didn't mean to interrupt."

"It's all right, Leon. My secretary was just showing me what she had made for me to wear for the initial television interview to open the trade fair. What do you think?"

Leaving the cart, his nephew stepped closer to examine everything. His brown eyes moved in fascination from one item to the other, then he looked at her with a dumbfounded expression.

"This is fabulous," he whispered. "You picked his namesake."

"I told you she was clever, Leon."

"But Uncle, this is really fantastic!" He kept looking at it, then at her.

"Do me another favor and try it on so I can see what I'll look like in it."

"That's a wonderful idea," Alex encouraged him. "You're almost the same height as your uncle. If something's wrong, I'll be able to get the alterations done in time."

He took the costume from her. "How did you know about Saint Dimitrios?"

"I love European art history."

"So do I! It's too bad you can't see some of the icons

and stained glass windows in the monasteries on Mount Athos.''

"That's the holy mountain where women aren't allowed.''

"You know that, too?''

She smiled. "I would suppose every woman who has studied Greece has heard of it. I think it's sad only men get to see its beauties. If it weren't for women, those monks would never have been given life in the first place.

"In fact I think it's sad they can't marry and worship at the same time. They miss out on so much. Can you imagine never watching the birth of your own baby?''

She'd said the last without thinking. Between the way Dimitrios's face darkened, combined with the hostile glance Leon suddenly flashed his uncle, she knew her words had been offensive to both men.

Leon's eyes slid away from hers. "If you'll both excuse me, I've just remembered something I have to do.'' He handed the things back to her and strode out of the room.

Alex felt sick.

Leon was always so polite and deferential in front of his uncle. For him to leave like that meant she'd really affronted him.

"I'm so sorry.''

"For what, Ms. Hamilton? Speaking your mind?''

She shook her head. "I'm the one who drove him away with my remarks. I meant no irreverence, but I'm sure that's how they sounded to him.'' *And you.*

"If you must know, he's at a crossroads in his life and feeling it. His hasty departure from the room had nothing to do with you. Personally I find your opinions refreshing. Now I think we'd better eat dinner before it grows cold. Perhaps by the time we've finished, Leon will come back to say good-night and we can prevail on him to model that fabulous costume for us.''

Dimitrios was doing his best to shield her because that was his nature, but it was clear her comments had upset both him and his nephew. What Alex would give if there'd been no accident. She'd be at the hotel right now where she belonged.

After laying the things on the end of the bed, she pushed the cart next to Dimitrios. All he had to do was put his feet on the floor. But her heart was heavy because she knew Leon wouldn't make another appearance tonight, at least not in front of her.

Even if it meant defying her boss, she would leave tomorrow morning to inspect the silk exhibits in Soufli. Being so close to Dimitrios had caused her to lose all perspective.

With the opening of the trade fair only two days away, she needed to focus on that and make sure everything was ready. Afterward, she would return to Thessalonica and check into the hotel.

She needed other people. Michael and his friends would provide laughter and camaraderie. As soon as Yanni arrived, he could join in. With their help she'd make it through this bittersweet experience. *She had no choice.*

CHAPTER FIVE

DIMITRIOS awoke the next morning feeling much more his old self. Although he was still sore here and there, the dizziness had pretty well disappeared.

He realized he hadn't been in his right mind for the last few days where his secretary had been concerned. Determined to reestablish professional distance with her, he started out the day by asking Serilda to send breakfast trays to their separate rooms.

Now that he'd showered and dressed, he was anxious to get to the office. He hoped Ms. Hamilton was ready to go.

When he entered the dining room looking for Leon, he found Ananke eating breakfast alone. He greeted her before asking why his nephew hadn't joined her. She looked at him with wounded eyes.

"Did you think he would stay around after the way you hurt him yesterday?"

He poured himself a cup of coffee from the buffet, then stood staring at her while he drank. "What exactly did he tell you?"

"That you had discussed his personal life with your secretary, and she'd had the nerve to offer her opinion as if it were her right!" Her voice shook. "You know how he adores you. How could you betray him like that?" she cried.

"Aside from the fact that I've never discussed Leon

with Ms. Hamilton, it might interest you to know she's on your side without realizing it.''

Ananke's eyes rounded. "What do you mean?"

In a few words he told her what had happened. "Her opinion obviously hit a nerve, otherwise he wouldn't have left the room so fast." As far as Dimitrios was concerned, it was exactly the kind of thing his nephew needed to hear before he made a final decision about his future.

"Nevertheless you can see why Leon's so upset," Ananke persisted. "Since you came from New York, you've been virtually inaccessible."

Even Ananke had picked up on his preoccupation with Ms. Hamilton. *Damn.* Well, that was over now.

He finished his coffee. "I recall spending part of yesterday afternoon with you and my nephew."

"But nothing was resolved!"

"We have to give him time to talk this out, Ananke. Maybe that's all he needs to realize this is a phase that will pass."

The irony of those words weren't wasted on Dimitrios when he considered his own alarming state of mind since he'd left New York. His interest in Ms. Hamilton better be a phase.

Ananke jumped up from the chair. "There's something different about you since your return."

No one knows that better than I do.

"If I'm different, it's because I'm feeling the weight of a father's responsibility without being a father. Perhaps it's time you knew that my brother never wanted to be a part of the family business, either."

She shook her head. "That's not true!"

"I wouldn't lie to you. Leon always preferred to be out-of-doors."

"Surely you're not saying he would rather have had a career in forestry than work for the Pandakis Corporation!" Her angry laugh resounded in the room.

"I have no idea how his life would have turned out had he lived." His voice grated. *Thanks to you, we'll never know.* "The point is, my nephew shows the same lack of interest in business as his father."

A stricken look crossed her face. "You're so cold, Dimitrios. Don't you care that he might leave us for good?"

"You already know the answer to that question. But forcing something that goes against his nature will only push him in the opposite direction that much faster."

"You wouldn't say that if he were *our* son."

"If Leon were my son and I'd been the one who'd died—" he spoke without acknowledging her attempt to personalize the situation "—I'd like to believe my brother would have listened to him, guided him as much as possible, then let him come to his own conclusions. Fortunately he hasn't made a definite decision yet."

He checked his watch. "We'll have to continue this conversation another time. My secretary and I need to get to the office."

"She already left."

His head reared back. The sudden movement reminded him of his recent head injury. "When?"

"I saw her leave in a taxi half an hour ago."

If he didn't miss his guess, Michael had asked her to come to the hotel room before her workday began. Dimitrios felt like he'd just been kicked in the gut.

"If Leon wants to talk, tell him to call me on my cell phone. I'll see you later."

He left the dining room and rang Kristofor to bring the car around. While he waited, he phoned his secretary on her cell phone. If the call came at an inopportune moment for her, he didn't particularly care.

To his surprise she answered on the second ring. "Hello?"

"Good morning, Ms. Hamilton."

"Mr. Pandakis. How are you feeling?" She sounded bright.

He gritted his teeth, trying to shut out certain pictures in his mind. "Well enough to be headed for my office. Shall I swing by the hotel and pick you up?"

"I—I didn't realize you meant to go into work today," she stammered.

Obviously not.

Attempting to tamp down his anger, he said, "Does that present a problem for you?"

"Actually it does."

Dimitrios inhaled sharply. "When can I expect you?"

"Tomorrow morning? You see, I was under the impression you needed to convalesce one more day, so I thought this would be the perfect time to visit Soufli and check out preparations. My flight's just been called."

"You're at the airport?" he demanded incredulously.

"Yes. It's one of those commuter planes we've advertised for the trade fair. After it lands in Alexandroupolis, I'll rent a car to drive the rest of the way. So far everything's working perfectly. If the car is at the airport waiting for me as I requested, then I don't foresee any problems for the fair attendees.

"I'll check each silk exhibition en route. In case there

are any glitches, we'll have time to sort them out tomorrow. I'll return on the first flight back to Thessalonica in the morning and report straight to your office.''

No boss could ask for more than that from his secretary. She gave a thousand percent all of the time. He had no right to be upset with her. No right at all.

''That's fine,'' he muttered, still trying to recover from the shock of realizing she wasn't anywhere in the villa. ''Keep in touch with me.''

''Yes, of course. I'm sorry, Mr. Pandakis, but I have to board now or they're going to close the gate. Goodbye.'' She clicked off.

Goodbye? Her cheery tone irritated the hell out of him.

If his secretary thought she'd seen the last of him until tomorrow, she had another think coming.

Using his phone once more, he canceled the car, then sent for the helicopter. While it was coming, he made one more call, to a lodge in Dadia requesting two rooms for the night. After that was accomplished, he returned to his bedroom for some additional clothes and his backpack.

One thing he knew about Ms. Hamilton. She would never lie to him, but that didn't mean she'd gone to Soufli alone. If joining her meant he interrupted something private, then so be it.

Alex walked through the Alexandroupolis terminal to the car rental counter where she'd arranged for transportation.

Everywhere she looked, whether in or outside the terminal, she saw flags and banners advertising the trade fair. It had been the same at the airport in Thessalonica.

There was a sense of festivity in the air that seemed to have affected everyone except her.

Two nights of living in close proximity to Dimitrios had created a physical ache for him that wasn't about to go away. For her own good, she'd wrenched herself from the villa early this morning in order not to see him.

She thought she'd escaped him until she'd heard his deep, familiar voice on the phone at the airport. Now she was in more pain than before. It was absolutely vital she leave her job the second the trade fair was over.

While waiting to board her flight, she'd phoned her mother to let her know she was all right. She'd kept their conversation brief. As for Michael, she'd finally been able to connect with him.

It sounded like he and the guys were having a terrific time. But when he wanted to talk about the costume and Dimitrios, she told him she had to go and would debrief after her return from Soufli.

"*Kalimera.* My name is Alex Hamilton. I requested a car?" She displayed her passport.

The employee was all smiles. "It's the black four-door right outside the building at the curb," he said in beautiful English. "You can't miss it because it has our company logo on the back window."

"Thank you." When nothing else was forthcoming she said, "May I have the key?"

"We have provided you with an English speaking driver."

"Oh. I had no idea."

She shouldn't have been surprised. The Pandakis name insured outstanding service. Dimitrios was a very special man, and no one knew that more than Alex.

There were women he dated who would have fought

to be first at his side had they known about the accident, yet he'd insisted on Alex's attentions. Looking after him all night had bonded her to him in a brand-new way.

But she had to face the fact that if he'd preferred her company for the last two nights, even over that of his own sister-in-law, it was because he'd known he didn't have to pretend in front of his secretary.

Dimitrios paid her a fantastic salary to do whatever was needed and place no demands on him. She might as well be another man for all the interest he took in her as a woman.

"Enjoy your trip to Soufli."

The man's parting comment brought her back from her torturous thoughts. "I'm sure I will."

With her suitcase in one hand, her briefcase in the other, she made her way out of the busy terminal.

As she approached the lane where a string of cars were idling, she noticed there were quite a few black ones mixed in with the others. Not certain which of them was hers, she started down the queue searching for the rental agency's logo.

"Alexandra?" came a vibrant male voice from behind her.

She spun around in surprise to hear her name, then almost fainted to discover who it was.

"Dimitrios—"

Alex had been thinking so hard about him, the word slipped out before she realized she'd said it. He was wearing sunglasses, a rare sight, but after his accident she assumed his eyes were still sensitive to the light.

"It's nice to hear you say my name," he drawled.

Suddenly she was out of breath. "I—I don't know what you mean."

His white smile dazzled her. "It's one thing to be formal in front of other people, but it's long past the time we functioned on a first name basis in private. Don't you agree?"

He took the cases from her hands and put them in the back seat of the car. While she watched, it dawned on her he was really here. To make things even more difficult for her, he was such an attractive Greek male, she couldn't look anywhere else.

The sage-colored summer suit with a white, open-necked silk shirt brought out the blackness of his hair and olive-toned skin. She had the overwhelming urge to hold him as she'd done on the plane when she'd cradled his head and shoulders in her lap.

"Why didn't you tell me you were coming while we were on the phone?" This wasn't the way this day was supposed to go, yet she was so thrilled to see him, she could hardly stand it.

"It was a last-minute decision. Rather than work at my office alone, I thought it might be more fun to join you while we both test the system for flaws." He opened the passenger door for her.

Fun?

Alex didn't know what to think. He'd teased her before, but never to this extent.

Averting her eyes, she climbed in the front seat. After he'd shut the door and had gone around to the driver's seat she asked, "Should you have flown anywhere this soon after your accident?"

He turned the key in the ignition, revving the engine. "Do I detect a note of pique in my secretary? I promise I won't bother you while we make our inspection."

"That isn't why I asked the question," she said in a

quiet voice. "I realize that without a command of your language, you were probably concerned I couldn't do this by myself. I just hope you won't suffer a relapse."

They pulled away from the curb and followed the exit signs. "If you're worried you'll have to nurse me half-way through the day, I promise I'm feeling fine."

"That's reassuring, especially when it's so close to the opening of the fair."

He didn't respond to her comment. Instead, he drove the car with the same expertise he did everything else. Before long they'd left the airport and were headed for Soufli, which according to her map was sixty-five kilometers away.

She sent him a furtive glance. It was still hard to believe he'd come all this distance when there were other things that needed his attention at his office.

He caught her looking at him. Her heart did a little kick. "Why did you bother to bring your suitcase, Alexandra?"

To hear him say her name with that slight trace of accent sent a ripple of forbidden excitement through her body.

"I didn't think I'd have enough time to visit all the exhibits and make it back to Thessalonica in one day, so I booked a room in Soufli for the night."

"Which hotel?"

"The Ilias."

"Considering the influx of tourists for the big event, I'm amazed they had anything available."

"I don't think they did. But as soon as I said your name, there was no problem."

At that remark he pulled his cell phone out of his suit jacket pocket and made a call. Except for words like hello and goodbye, it was impossible to follow his Greek. Curious to know who he was phoning, she waited for an explanation after he clicked off, but it never came.

Finally she couldn't stand it any longer. "Is everything all right?"

"It is now," came the mysterious reply.

She hated it when he refused to explain his actions, particularly in this case because she was afraid they had something to do with her. In order to get her mind off him, she studied her map. It was printed on the brochure the man at the car rental desk had given her when he'd handed back her passport.

"You see that little area outside Soufli?" He touched the spot with his index finger.

At his close proximity, she drew in an unsteady breath. "Yes."

"That's called Dadia. We'll be sleeping there tonight."

She bit the inside of her lip. "Have you forgotten the government dinner at the Dodona Palace this evening? I accepted for you a month ago."

"On my way here I told them I needed another twenty-four hours to convalesce from my accident. My cousin Vaso is going to attend in my place."

Alex turned her head to look out the side window. No matter which member of the illustrious Pandakis family was sent, the officials would be disappointed because it was Dimitrios they wanted. Instead, he was going to be with *her*.

If he didn't have worries about her being able to get around the country without his help, then the only other reason she could imagine him showing up like this was that he needed a legitimate excuse to put space between him and his nephew.

Maybe there'd been another unpleasant episode with Leon this morning, and Dimitrios hadn't recovered enough to deal with it yet. Ananke Pandakis hadn't said more than two words to her at breakfast.

Alex had wanted to ask the other woman to tell Leon how sorry she was for having offended him with her insensitive remarks. But the negative tension radiating from his mother had made conversation impossible. As soon as the taxi arrived, Alex had been only too glad to slip away from the villa.

"What should we do about the Ilias?"

"Don't worry. I canceled your reservation."

"Some desperate tourist is going to be very happy."

"But not you?"

He was playing the relentless inquisitor again. When he was like this, there was no stopping him.

"I'm perfectly content to spend the night anywhere, you know that. Is there something special about Dadia?"

"It's the forest that's famous. As a boy, I explored every centimeter of it with my brother."

"Your favorite place?" She couldn't help asking. His love of mountaineering must have been born there.

He nodded. "I've been back several times, but I haven't climbed to the top of Gibrena Peak since my brother Leonides died."

He'd spoken of his brother's death to Mrs. Landau, but this was the first time he'd mentioned it to Alex. Moved by his tone, her hands clutched together. "You'll see it through different eyes this time."

"That's true. You can't return and expect things to be the same. But knowing you and your passion for life, I shall enjoy watching your reaction. Tell me now if you didn't bring suitable clothing. There's a store in the village we're coming to where we can buy what you need.''

Panic gripped Alex in its vise.

''I—I didn't bring any walking clothes to Greece.''

''No problem.''

Perspiration broke out on her hairline. ''Why don't you drop me off in Soufli to do my work? It will leave you free to visit your old haunt unencumbered. We can meet at the silk mansion in the morning for the trip back.''

''Have you forgotten your hotel room is gone?''

She shifted in the seat. ''I'll find something else.''

''It's already noon. Too late in the day to make other arrangements.''

''Is it very steep in the forest?''

''I suppose that all depends on your definition of the word steep.''

''Can I explore it in this outfit and my sneakers, or are you talking about scaling walls?''

Deep-throated laughter rumbled out of him. ''I'm not asking you to climb a mountain.''

''That's good.'' She could have wept in relief. ''A picture of all those plaques and trophies in your closet flashed before my eyes. It almost gave me a heart attack.''

''So that explains why you took so long to find the garment bag.'' He was still chuckling.

Heat filled her cheeks. ''I admit I'm a bit of a snoop.''

''I prefer to call it an inquiring mind. It's what makes you an irreplaceable secretary. If I haven't said it before, you've redefined the word for me, and I'm indebted to you, Alexandra.''

Whenever he said her name, he made it sound so beautiful.

"Thank you," she whispered in agony. A nagging voice cried, *Is it worth it to be the bridesmaid, but never the bride?*

"Tomorrow will be soon enough to inspect the exhibits. Today I'd like to reward you for all your hard work by showing you a national treasure. How does that appeal to you?"

Oh, Dimitrios. If you only knew. "That sounds lovely."

Convinced she'd arranged to spend the night with her American boyfriend, Dimitrios should have felt guilty for thwarting her plans. But heaven help him, all he could feel was a sense of elation that they were going to be alone together far from the horde.

Since they'd been driving, he hadn't heard her cell phone ring. For that matter, she hadn't tried to use it. He was surprised she didn't want to stop at a local shop, if only to excuse herself long enough to make contact with Michael.

Of course she could have planned to get in touch with him later in the day. Then again, maybe she was meeting her Greek boyfriend, and Michael didn't have a clue.

Dimitrios grimaced at the thoughts assailing him.

Was it possible Yanni had flown up from Athens? Why not enjoy a private interlude with her before she had to return to Thessalonica where her other lover was waiting for her at the hotel.

Did both men resent the time Dimitrios demanded of

her? The late nights at his office? The early-morning conferences?

He wondered how Michael felt about having to pick up the costume she'd had made for him, let alone be asked to bring it all the way to Greece on the plane.

Had it upset him to learn she'd be staying at the villa instead of the hotel? Or was he so sure of her, it would never occur to him to worry what she was doing with her employer.

If Dimitrios were in either man's shoes, the thought of her making love to anyone but him caused a blackness to sweep over him. The feeling was so staggering, so powerful, it took him a minute to recognize it for what it was.

"Shouldn't we have taken that turnoff for Dadia?" Her voice seemed to come from far away.

"There'll be another one in a minute," he muttered, still gripped by the sheer force of emotion too painfully raw for him to shake off. Jealousy had never touched his life until now.

"Oh, Dimi—listen to me. You're barely twelve. Not quite old enough for a man's feelings to have taken over inside you yet. When that day comes, your body will react when you see a beautiful woman. You'll want to hold her, make love to her. The pleasure a woman can bring you is to die for."

Dimitrios struggled to control his rapid breathing.

The night she'd brushed those magic fingers of hers across his forehead had brought him pleasure to die for. The thought of those same fingers on his body tonight…

Lord. He was already so far out of control where she was concerned, he didn't know what in the hell he was going to do about the situation. He'd made reservations for two rooms, but the way he was feeling right now, one of them would be going to waste. Dimitrios couldn't believe he'd reached this point.

"Your cell phone's ringing," she reminded him.

There was no way he could talk to anyone right now. He handed it to her. "When you answer it, tell whoever it is I'll get back to them."

"It's coming from the villa. What if it's your nephew?"

She knew him too well. But the question drew his attention to the generous curve of her lips with their flare of passion.

When he'd awakened the morning after the accident to find her face mere inches from his, he remembered thinking she had a mouth nature had made without flaw.

"Shall I let it ring?"

He rubbed the back of his neck. "If it's Leon, I'll talk to him."

Except that as he listened, it became clear someone else had called. The conversation was over so fast, he realized it had to have been Ananke. These days she was so upset over Leon, she'd forgotten her manners.

After his secretary had clicked off she said, "That was your sister-in-law. She told me to tell you her son is no longer a student at the university. He just left the villa with his backpack and indicated he wouldn't be around for the family dinner tomorrow night."

That didn't surprise him. It was a knee-jerk reaction to punish Dimitrios for taking Alexandra into his confidence, or so Leon had thought. "What else did she say?"

"That was all, but she sounded...desolate." Her head

swerved in his direction. "I got the distinct impression she blames me that he's gone away so upset."

He changed into a lower gear so the car could begin its gradual ascent to the lodge. "My sister-in-law's one dream has been to see her son rise to the head of the Pandakis Corporation. What she forgot to remember is that Leon is capable of dreaming his own dreams.

"Whether they have substance or not, he thinks he wants to be a monk on Mount Athos. She's terrified of losing him."

"Oh, dear God— I'm so sorry—" The voice of the woman next to him shook with pain.

"Don't fall apart on me now, Alexandra. For him to run away because you happened to express an innocent opinion in his presence means he's more childish and immature than I thought."

She shook her head. "That's not it. He must have believed you'd confided his dream to me, a mere secretary. He couldn't help but think I was trying to influence him on your behalf. If I'd been in his shoes, I would have felt a trust had been broken, too."

Dimitrios had to clear his throat, not only because of her understanding and sensitivity of the problem, but because of her earnestness in trying to make him understand how badly she felt.

"He worships you!" she cried. "I saw it in his eyes and expression the moment he boarded the plane and found you suffering. And later at the villa, until I ruined everything, he was so excited to try on the costume for you."

"I love him very much, and appreciate what you're

saying, but I'm not blind to the fact that he's still very young for his age.''

"Age doesn't matter when you're not used to sharing the person you love with a stranger,'' she came back. "I don't blame Ananke for being beside herself. If I could just tell Leon you bear no fault in this.''

"I appreciate your defense of me, Alexandra, but if my nephew can't see how petty he's being, then he's not ready to make life-changing decisions.''

"I think it's more a case of his being afraid he could never measure up to you. Perhaps he sees the monastery as a place where he won't have to try.''

He marveled at her ability to see through to the heart of a situation. Her mind was as exciting as everything else about her.

"My uncle Spiros used coercion on everyone in the family in order to have his will obeyed. Even my own father gave in to him out of fear. When I became Leon's guardian, I determined that was the one thing I would never do.''

"Perhaps you succeeded so well, it has led him to believe you don't think he's capable of following in your footsteps. Maybe it's your approval he's been waiting for to give him that final push in the right direction, but he never received it. If that's the case, then my comments to him would have come as a double blow.''

"What do you mean?'' Her understanding was rather astounding. He found himself anxious to hear what else she had to say.

"Have you told him straight out you don't want him to be a monk?''

"No.''

"Why not?"

"Because it's possible he has a true vocation."

"But don't you see—" She broke off talking.

He turned his head toward her. "Go on."

"I—I'm much too outspoken. It's none of my business."

"After what happened in my bedroom, I'd say you're very much involved. Finish what you were going to tell me."

She was making more sense than anyone he'd ever known. With every word that came from her mouth, he found himself more enamored of her.

"Maybe he took my remarks to mean that you don't think he'd make a very good monk, either. Coming from me, it must have been humiliating for him."

Good heavens. Was it possible she had hit on the truth?

He couldn't count the number of times Ananke had begged him to take Leon in hand. But all these years he'd shut his mind and heart to her entreaties because *she'd* been the one doing the pleading.

From the moment Leonides had told him he'd been trapped into a loveless marriage, Ananke had been emotionally dead to Dimitrios.

If Alexandra was even partially correct, then he'd done a terrible disservice to his nephew, who could be floundering. It made sense he'd gone off to lick his wounds.

Dimitrios struggled to contain emotions erupting inside him. To think Alexandra had applied for a job with him four years ago, yet only now was he beginning to understand what a true prize she was.

Without wasting any more time, he reached for the

phone to call Leon, but his nephew had turned off his cell phone. The only thing to do was leave a message.

"Leon?" he spoke in Greek. "Wherever you are, I hope you hear this in time. I thought I was recovered enough from my accident to take part in the opening ceremony of the trade fair. But I flew in the helicopter to inspect the silk exhibits and found out I'm still too dizzy to contemplate anything that vigorous.

"I need you home, preferably by tomorrow afternoon. Thank goodness for all the polo you played. You ride like you were born in the saddle. We can also be grateful you inherited your father's height and build. Besides me, you're the only other man in the family who could wear that costume Ms. Hamilton went to so much trouble to have made.

"You'll be leading the parade with a regiment of mounted soldiers. That means giving a speech on horseback while you're in front of the dignitaries' stand. You're the only Pandakis I'd trust to face the media with their cameras.

"After the many talks we've had, you know how important this trade fair is. I have every confidence you'll make all of Greece proud, especially your mother who has raised such a fine son."

Dimitrios could admit that much about Ananke. She'd been devoted to Leon.

"If you hear this message before I get home tomorrow afternoon, phone me and we'll talk."

He clicked off, anxious to find out what kind of response he would get from his nephew, if any. At least he'd taken the first step to rectify a situation he may have unwittingly created years ago. Unfortunately it might be too late if Leon had already shut down. Only time would tell.

Thanks to the wisdom of the woman seated next to him, Dimitrios had been given a fighting chance to make amends.

Right now he felt an urgency to get her strictly alone with him. What better spot than the pristine forest that lay ahead of them.

CHAPTER SIX

ALEX didn't know what Dimitrios had said to his nephew. But the expression on his face revealed a world of love and concern.

After he put the phone back in his pocket he said, "If Leon hears my message, he'll be under the impression I'm still too dizzy to ride in the parade. I told him he was the only Pandakis I trusted to stand in for me at the opening ceremony. We'll find out if he takes the bait."

She looked out the side window so he couldn't see her blinking back the tears. There were many ways to love a man. At sixteen, he'd been her handsome knight in shining armor who'd come to rescue her.

After she'd gone to work for his company, she'd learned to love him for his generosity to the staff. When she became his private secretary, she fell in love with his little foibles along with his most endearing traits. Above all, she admired that selfless quality about him which was rare in a man so influential.

Right now her heart was swollen with emotion because he hadn't been too proud to find a way to reach out to his troubled nephew.

The man had no vanity.

Alex loved him with a searing intensity that needed to find expression soon or she'd go mad trying to hold back her feelings.

She continued to stare out the window as the car wound through a small village on its climb to a more forested area. They passed a tiny white church sheltered by dark pines. There were cars all around it and a few people outside the doors in native dress. It had to be some kind of religious celebration.

She was on the verge of asking Dimitrios about it when he announced they'd come to the lodge.

Alex turned her head to the other side of the road in time to see a cluster of white buildings nestled in the trees. It looked deserted.

"After we've freshened up and changed, we'll walk to the top of the peak. From there you'll be able to see over the entire forest."

In such a remote place, this was going to be even more intimate than her stay at the villa.

"How long will it take?"

"The rest of the day." He drove up to the front of one of the buildings, which appeared to house a dining room. After he'd shut off the motor he said, "Is there a reason you're in such a hurry?"

A wry tone had entered his voice. Whenever he sounded like that, she knew he was probing for something. *But what?*

"Not at all. I just wondered if it might be too soon for you to exert yourself to that extent."

Her explanation was part lie, of course. Any time spent alone with him was too long because she kept falling deeper and deeper in love. On the other hand, she *was* worried that he hadn't fully recovered yet.

"Nothing relaxes me more than to get out in nature." He pulled off his sunglasses, revealing those penetrating black eyes to her gaze for the first time that day. "We both need a break from the stress before the fair begins."

So saying, he levered himself from the car and came

around to help her. When they went inside the reception area, the lodge keeper rushed to greet Dimitrios in Greek. He obviously knew him well.

While they conversed at some length, the man's wife brought them tea and biscuits. The repast tasted good. After they'd finished, she bid Alex to follow her from the office to one of the nearby cottages.

It turned out to be a pleasant room with an ensuite bathroom and three twin beds. Dimitrios came inside with her suitcase. He tipped the woman, then shut the door behind her.

Turning to Alex, he pinned her with his dark, level gaze. "I arranged for two rooms before I left Thessalonica this morning. However, the concierge just informed me that a problem has arisen and now there's only this one available. Apparently the granddaughter of the concierge and his wife is being married today, and they're expecting more family."

"In that little church we just passed?" she cried in delight.

He nodded. "The wedding party is staying here for the night, so the lodge is closed to the public."

She smiled to herself. "But there's always a room for you."

"Because I serve on the eco council for special preserves like this throughout Greece, an accommodation is usually made available if a member is in the area."

He served on many boards, but being his New York assistant, she hadn't heard of this one. It seemed that every day in his presence meant she learned something new about him.

"*How* special?"

His eyes gleamed. "If we're lucky, you're going to

find out. Don't worry about tonight. I brought my bed-roll. After we have dinner, I plan to sleep in the forest. Excuse me for a moment and I'll bring in my things.''

Once he left the room, Alex stood there immobilized with fresh pain.

Given the unexpected circumstances, any other man might have tried to take advantage of the situation. Not Dimitrios. The night of the accident he'd wanted her to stay with him to help run interference. But now that he was recovered, it didn't occur to him to ask her to share the room with him.

She had to admit it wasn't anyone's fault but hers. Michael had created this persona for her. One that made her blend into the woodwork.

Alex blended all right. So well, in fact, that Dimitrios saw her as one of the guys. She could be Stavros for all he cared.

Of course he cared a great deal for his Greek secretary. She knew Dimitrios cared a lot for her, too. Wanting to show her a favorite place of his meant they'd become friends. *But never lovers.*

Back in high school and college she'd dated quite a bit, but because she'd lost her heart to a certain Greek, no other man had ever meant enough to her to become intimate with him.

Tonight that was what she wanted. To lie in his arms and get so intimate with him, he would never let her go.

But if she dared shed her disguise right now in order to make him see her in a different light, it would end their friendship. He would despise her for misrepresenting herself to get a job with his corporation. Everything would blow up in her face. It was going to blow up anyway after she resigned.

The mere thought of never seeing him again was anathema to her. She couldn't imagine getting through the rest of her life without him, yet the day of parting was almost here. There was nothing she could do now but play this out to the bitter end.

Stifling a tiny sob, she hurried into the bathroom with her suitcase. After freshening up, she pulled out the plastic bag holding her sneakers. Once she'd slipped off her matron pumps, she put on her navy and white tennis shoes.

They didn't match her three-piece, oversize suit with the high square neck. It was an unattractive jacquard design of intricately woven salmon pink, gray and brown. During the hike she imagined she'd get hot wearing it, but that would have to be her punishment.

When she finally went into the room, the sight of his powerful body in cutoffs and a white T-shirt revealing the well-defined chest beneath caused her to suck in her breath.

On the same note, his eyes passed over her with less interest than if he'd glimpsed a plate of fried eggs left out on the table for the better part of a week.

How awful she looked. It killed her to go on wearing such unattractive clothes in front of him, never being able to let down her hair and be herself. Just once she'd like to see those black orbs ignite when she walked into a room....

He hung his suit in the closet, then reached for his backpack. It was sheer poetry watching his bronzed, hard-muscled arms slip into the straps.

"What have you got inside?" she inquired. "It looks heavy."

"This is nothing. Some food and water plus a few

other items. Shall we go?'' He locked the door behind them.

For the next twenty minutes she followed him along a path, which started to wind into foothills studded with black pine and oak. ''Are we on sacred ground yet?''

Dimitrios paused to look back at her with an amused smile that tripled her pulse rate. ''We'll be coming to the strictly protected area before too long. When you see something move, I'll give you the binoculars.''

Startled, she said, ''I'd settle for a clue about now.''

His lips twitched. ''That would spoil all the fun.''

Uh-oh. This outing seemed to have brought out the boy in him. She had an idea she was in for it.

He handed her a bottle of water from his pack. ''Don't drink too much all at once,'' he cautioned.

After a moment she returned it and they resumed their trek. He continued along the path, pacing himself so Alex could keep up. Though the scenery was beautiful, she found herself watching the backs of his legs. They were perfectly molded machines of whipcord strength.

Content to feast her eyes on Dimitrios, she almost bumped into him when he stopped ten minutes later to point out a family of badgers partially hidden by the underbrush. Alex took a step off the path to get a closer peek at them. They were burrowing for all their worth.

''Oh—look how hard they're working!''

''They remind me of you.''

The mocking comparison to the grizzle-coated mammals was hardly flattering, but she'd come to recognize his mockery as a compliment of sorts.

''Thank you very much.''

She thought she heard a chuckle as they continued up the path. The higher they rose, the more she became aware of a forest alive with the sounds of rustlings and whirrings. No doubt foxes and other creatures abounded in the wooded setting.

They stopped to drink more water. When he'd put the bottle away, he took out the binoculars. Before she knew how it happened, he'd hung them around her neck.

In the process, his hands brushed her hair and shoulders, setting her on fire wherever there was contact. She quickly averted her eyes, afraid to look at him.

"We're getting closer to the peak. Keep your gaze skyward."

She nodded, unable to talk with his body practically touching hers, radiating his male warmth. Once he'd turned and started up the trail again, she was able to expel the breath she'd been holding.

They hadn't been hiking more than five minutes before she saw several dark specks in the sky. With each leisurely circle, they came closer.

She took off her glasses and lifted the binoculars to her eyes. Unprepared for the powerful magnification of the lenses, she gasped in shock at the incredible sight.

"I don't believe it! They look like gargoyles come to life! I've never seen anything like them."

"You're viewing a pair of Griffon vultures," sounded her companion's deep voice. "They would be extinct by now if there weren't forest preserves like this to provide needed habitat. Along with the Black and Egyptian vultures, they're one of the most endangered species of raptors in the world."

"No wonder you love to come here! I feel like I've gone back in time. I wish I had my sketch pad with me."

"Wait till you see the Imperial eagle."

"Is that the one you have emblazoned on your plane?" She was still looking through the field glasses.

"So you noticed." He sounded pleased.

I notice everything about you.

"Well, it didn't look like an American bald eagle, so I figured it had special significance."

"You don't miss much."

Not when it comes to you.

"Once when Leonides brought me here, we found an Imperial eaglet that had been poisoned. We notified the authorities and they took it to the bird hospital. After it recovered, we were allowed to watch it from the observatory when it was returned."

She swallowed hard. "That must have pleased you both."

"We were very happy. My brother felt it was important to fight for their preservation."

"So you took up the cause. What a perfect way to honor his memory." She handed him back the binoculars and put her glasses on. "Does your nephew know about that story?"

He stared at her with brooding eyes. "No. In the beginning, I found it too painful a subject to talk about. I realize it's another oversight I intend to rectify if it isn't already too late."

"I don't imagine it's ever too late for a son to hear something truly wonderful about his father."

She saw his throat move before they continued the last of their climb side by side.

"You had a happy childhood, didn't you, Alexandra."

"My parents are loving people who gave me and my sisters a wonderful life."

"Is that the reason why you don't talk about it around

me? Because you've learned enough to know mine was less than idyllic?''

No. It was the fear of loving him too much when she knew it was one-sided that kept her silent, but she couldn't let him know that. With his all-seeing gaze focused on her, she started to feel nervous.

"I guess I've been too busy being your secretary to realize much of anything else. Where did you say that observatory was?'' Their conversation was getting too personal.

"Along another path. It'll be closed today, but we have our own binoculars and can stop there on our way down to watch the raptors feed.''

The next three hours were sheer delight for Alex. They ate by the ruins of a Byzantine castle on top of the peak, then made their descent. Dimitrios identified fifteen endangered species for her, including the Imperial eagle.

Almost at the bottom, she thought she heard music and stopped along the trail to listen.

"It's the wedding party. See that little meadow through the trees? They must have arrived from the village church.''

Her breath caught in her throat to witness the joy of a radiant bride in her wedding dress with a crown of flowers in her hair, dancing with her dark-haired groom.

In the background their friends and relatives clapped and cheered to the music while the little children played.

Tears sprang to Alex's eyes. "I've never seen anything so beautiful.''

The scene before her was too painful to watch because she wanted to be that bride smiling into her husband's eyes. She wanted that wedding to be her wedding. She wanted Dimitrios for her husband. To have and to hold. Forever.

"I agree that village weddings tend to have a certain charm," he murmured. "Come stand over here where we can see better."

Needing to touch her, he grasped her shoulders from behind and moved her off the path where they could remain hidden behind the undergrowth to watch. But it was a mistake.

There was no way he could focus on the bridal party when the intoxicating scent of pear from her shampoo made him want to take down her hair and bury his face in it.

Like before, on the plane, Dimitrios was aware of the superb mold of her body. Considering the eighty-degree heat, it came as a shock to discover she was trembling. He knew she wasn't afraid of him. Was it desire she felt for him?

If that were the case, then her struggle to conceal it made her different from all the other females who'd come on to him since his teens. She was that rare woman he never expected to meet.

Earlier that morning he'd awakened full of determination to keep her at a professional distance. Yet here he was, held in the grip of sexual desire, wanting to turn her around so he could kiss her senseless.

He knew he should be feeling guilty for spending time with her in activities that had nothing to do with business. For that matter, he should never have insisted she stay at the villa. But it was too late for that now, too late to remember the vow that no woman would entice him to bed before marriage.

He wanted, needed Alexandra in all the ways a man could want a woman. He'd fallen in love with her....

"I—I hope you don't mind if we hurry back to the lodge now. All of a sudden I'm fading fast." She eased away from him and started down the path.

Dimitrios followed at a more leisurely pace, wondering if guilt over betraying Michael or Yanni had caused her to put distance between them. Determined to find out, he closed the gap.

"You're reading my mind again. An early night is exactly what I need, too."

She slowed down before darting him a backward glance. "Are you feeling dizzy?"

"No. Only pleasantly tired."

"Somehow I don't quite believe you. Thank goodness the lodge isn't very far now. That backpack must feel heavy."

He waited for her to say he could lean on her, but the offer didn't come.

Because she didn't trust herself to get that close to him again?

Desperate to know the answer to that vital question, an idea came to him how he could discover the truth.

Filled with a sense of anticipation for the evening ahead, Dimitrios walked her toward the lodge. The pines cast their long shadows across the path. His heart thudded to realize evening had crept up on them without him realizing it. He would have her all to himself.

It didn't matter that there were cars in every parking space. The wedding guests would stay occupied for hours, leaving him and Alexandra strictly alone.

"Do you mind if I stretch out for a few minutes?" he asked as soon as he let them inside the room.

She looked at him in alarm. "Are you feeling sick? Sometimes a cola helps. I could ask for one at the lodge."

He loved it that she showed this kind of concern for him. It staggered him how much he loved her.

Shaking his head, he said, "I'm sleepy. That's all. If you want to shower, go ahead. The concierge said they'd bring dinner to our room. I'll call the office now."

After putting his backpack on one of the chairs, he laid down on one of the twin beds and picked up the receiver to order their meal. Through veiled eyes he watched her reach for her suitcase.

"I'll hurry," she murmured before disappearing.

The second he heard the shower, he called Stavros for a short chat on his cell phone, then listened for any messages. So far there was no response from Leon. He hoped by morning he'd hear from his nephew.

His eyes flicked to the radio on the table between the beds. He turned it to a popular music station, curious to know Alexandra's taste. With the curtains drawn and the lights turned low, there was nothing else to do but wait for her. He couldn't think of anything else more important.

The shower had felt wonderful, but Alex stood before the mirror in a panic.

It had grown dark. Before long it would be time for bed. She couldn't go out there in front of him wearing another three-piece suit. But to suddenly appear in jeans and a T-shirt would be disastrous.

When she'd packed for this trip, it never occurred to her she might need a granny gown. All she'd thought to bring with her were some shortie nighties. Her robe was a simple yellow brushed nylon that fell to the knee and looked too youthful compared to the other things she'd been wearing to work.

Of course if she didn't use the belt, and wore one of her heavy white blouses and a half slip beneath it, she'd be able to conceal her figure. Alex hadn't brought slippers, but she'd packed a clean pair of white socks. In a moment she'd pulled them on.

Once her glasses were in place, she left the bathroom with her suitcase.

"I'm sorry if I took too—"

But she didn't finish what she was going to say because everything had changed since she'd been in the shower.

Her gaze shot to the square table, which had been set with candles and flowers. Dimitrios stood next to it filling two tall stemmed glasses with wine. She could smell something delicious. Greek music played in the background.

When he'd ordered dinner, she hadn't expected all this! Her heart couldn't take anymore.

Dimitrios turned toward her. In the flickering candlelight, his eyes gleamed like polished jet. He looked amazingly refreshed. "Leave your bag there and join me."

Once she'd done his bidding, she crossed the expanse on legs that had turned to jelly. He held the chair while she sat down. What was going on?

He took his place across the table from her and lifted his wineglass. "Shall we drink a toast to the fair?"

Trying not to look at him for fear he'd see the love in her eyes, she raised her glass. "May it be the success you envisioned."

"Amen."

They clinked glasses before he drank from his.

Alex rarely touched alcohol, but she needed something to steady her nerves, and the wine was very sweet to the taste. Unfortunately she swallowed too much, too fast. Grabbing the napkin, she coughed into it. "I'm sorry," came her muffled apology.

As he removed the covers off their dinner plates, a faint smile curved the corners of his mouth. "Perhaps this wedding fare will go down more easily."

She took a bite of the roast lamb and found it as delicious as everything else. But her awareness of the man seated opposite her had taken away her appetite.

Something was different. *He* was different. By his behavior, she could almost believe he was attracted to her, too. *Dear God.* Was it possible? Or had her desire for him grown to such a degree she saw only what she wanted to see?

"If the food isn't to your taste, I can go to the village for fruit and a sandwich." By now he'd practically devoured everything on his plate.

"Oh, no— I mean, that isn't the problem, but thank you anyway."

His gaze scrutinized her. "If you'd shed your jacket during the climb, you wouldn't have overheated."

"I'm fine. It's simply a case of my being more sleepy than hungry."

"Alexandra, you needn't pretend with me."

Her head reared back. "What do you mean?"

"I realize you were planning to spend your free evenings with Michael. So far I've claimed all your time."

She blinked. It hadn't occurred to her he would think she was romantically involved with Michael. Yet what else would he assume considering she'd offered to let Michael stay in her hotel room.

That put a different complexion on things. She hated the idea of deceiving Dimitrios any more than she already had.

"Michael knows my work for you comes first."

He finished off the rest of his wine. "Is that what you're going to tell him? That it was all work?"

"If he should ask, naturally I'll be honest with him."

"And he won't be jealous?"

"Heavens, no! You're my boss."

He sat back in his chair eyeing her narrowly. "If you were my girlfriend, I wouldn't allow you to spend a whole day with your employer in the woods."

Alex couldn't help smiling despite the pain she was feeling inside.

"My remark amused you?" He sounded anything but pleased.

"Today's woman doesn't consider herself a man's property. But the truth is, if I were Michael's girlfriend, I wouldn't have chosen to spend my free time with you, even if you do pay my salary."

There! She'd told him the truth.

"Does Michael know you're not his girlfriend?" He persisted in the same vein.

"Did he say something to Leon when he went for the costume that led him to believe we're more than good friends?"

"Not that I'm aware of," came the silky response.

Dimitrios was after a certain answer. She wished she knew was it was. Unless—

"It was probably one of Michael's friends playing a joke."

Her host's dark brows furrowed. "I don't follow."

"Michael's an old friend of mine who brought two of his buddies to Greece with him. One of them is divorced. Michael and the other one are between girlfriends at the moment.

"They work in the day and act in the theater at night. When they heard about the fair and the idea of wearing costumes, they were so excited to come, I told them they could stay in my suite. There weren't any more rooms to be had, and I knew I wouldn't be using it except to sleep."

She hoped that was the end of the questions. Alex reached for her wine and drank most of the contents.

"What about Yanni?"

She almost choked again. "I don't understand."

"Is he planning to stay in your suite, too?"

Alex put the glass on the table, wondering when the interrogation was going to stop.

"Yes. He went to Athens first to be with his family. From what I understand, he's bringing a girl along I've never met. As far as I know, they haven't arrived in Thessalonica yet."

"It all sounds very cozy," he murmured. "I wonder what would be your response if I asked to sleep over, too."

It was a teasing comment, but at the mere thought, her heart leaped. "Everyone would love it."

"Even you?"

Dimitrios. He sounded very much like a man who cared. If by some miracle that were true…

"Naturally it would be worth it to see the look on their faces. They wouldn't believe the legendary Kyrie Pandakis came down from Olympus to—"

Oh, no!

"Go on."

"I—I don't remember what I was going to say," she dissembled. The wine had made her careless.

"Maybe it will come to you while I'm in the shower."

CHAPTER SEVEN

AFTER Dimitrios had left the room, she decided the best thing she could do to get rid of the light-headed feeling was eat her dinner. Without him torturing her with questions, she found her appetite had returned.

Now that everything was out in the open concerning the friends staying at the hotel with her, she felt a lot better.

Once she'd finished her meal, she put the covers on the plates. As she blew out the candles, Dimitrios emerged from the bathroom wearing a pair of gray sweats and another T-shirt in pale blue. He brought the tang of soap into the room with him.

She noticed that his black hair was still damp from the shower, but he hadn't taken the time to shave. The shadow of a beard made him look so dark and handsome, she could only stare at him.

His gaze swept over her, igniting her senses all over again. "I don't know about you, but watching that bridal couple has put me in the mood to dance. Would you honor me with one before I leave you in peace?"

Dance? With her? When she'd never looked worse in her life?

Her boss probably knew she was in love with him. Maybe he'd known it all along and had decided to give his old-maid secretary a few thrills while she was in Greece. Let her have a memory to take back to New York.

116

"Something you have to learn about the Greek male. He loves to dance." Dimitrios put out his hands. "Indulge me."

Delicious waves of excitement raced through her body. Maybe her dream to become unforgettable to him was starting to come true. Her legs almost buckled as she dared to imagine he might really want to hold her close. "I don't think—"

"This is one time when I don't want you to think, Alexandra. Just go with the music. The bouzouki is too compelling to ignore."

"I don't know any Greek dances," she grumbled.

But her declaration had no effect on him as he drew her resisting body into his arms.

"All you have to do is relax," he whispered near her ear. After he'd removed her glasses and put them on the bed, he held her close enough that she could follow his lead.

Earlier she'd practically melted to feel his broad chest against her back. Now that her curves were melded to his rock-hard physique, her bones turned to liquid every time their legs brushed against each other.

Zeus in her arms.

She didn't dare let this go on any longer.

"I think we'd better stop. You've had enough activity for one day."

"I'll live to see another."

As if to make his point, he pulled her closer and moved her around the room with practised ease.

"Dimitrios," she begged.

"I like it when you say my name. I like being with you. Admit you enjoy my company, too." She felt his deep voice resonate to every cell in her sensitized body.

"If that weren't true, I wouldn't have worked for you all these years."

"A man likes to hear the words once in a while, even from his secretary."

"Well, now that you've been given your wish, I really must insist we stop. We have a big day ahead of us tomorrow."

"So we do."

He stopped moving his legs, but continued to rock her in place. "Thank you for the dance, Alexandra. It was exactly what the doctor ordered."

His hands seemed to slide away reluctantly, leaving her bereft. "I'll see you in the morning. Be sure to lock the door after me." He reached for his backpack.

"Wait," she cried.

"Yes?" He paused at the entrance.

"Where's your sleeping bag?"

"In the trunk of the car."

"What if you should become ill during the night?"

He shot her an enigmatic glance. "It isn't going to happen."

"But it could!" After their hike, she was fearful he might have overdone things. "I don't think I'll get any sleep tonight knowing you're out there somewhere in the forest where you might suffer a dizzy spell and no one would be there to help you."

He rubbed his jaw absently. "If you're that concerned, then I'll sleep in the car outside the cottage door."

"No!" she cried. "You're too big and you need a good night's rest," she stammered. "Stay in here. It isn't as if we haven't spent all night in the same bedroom before. That way if you're sick, I'll be here to help you."

She could read nothing from his expression. "That's very generous of you. If you're sure—"

"Of course." Once again she disappeared into the bathroom.

With pounding heart, he turned off the lamp and slid under the covers. When his adorable secretary finally emerged, his hungry gaze followed her silhouette as she got in her bed and purposely rolled away from him.

One dance with her and a fire had been lit that wasn't about to go out. He could still feel her delectable body pressed against him. In fact he was dangerously close to joining her in her bed.

The cell phone rang. Smothering a groan of frustration, he reached for it and clicked on.

"*Yassou.*" He spoke in Greek.

"Uncle?"

Relief swept over Dimitrios. "Leon, thank goodness. Where are you right now?"

"With Nikos."

"He's a good friend."

After a brief silence, "You shouldn't have left the villa until you were better," he blurted in a voice of chastisement, which was very touching.

"I found that out earlier today. Fortunately I'm in bed now."

"Where?"

"At the lodge on the edge of the Dadia forest."

"With Ms. Hamilton?"

He sucked in his breath. "Yes."

"Mother told me I jumped to conclusions about your confiding in her. I'm sorry. It was rude of me to walk out on you like that."

"There's no need for apologies. It was a misunderstanding all the way around."

"What are you doing in Dadia?"

"Reliving a memory I have of your father. I should have shared it with you years ago, but when he died, I was in so much pain, I shut off emotionally."

"Uncle Vaso told me you two were really close."

"Very. When your grandparents were killed, Leonides became mother, father and brother to me. After his death, I suffered. Then you were born, and it was like having my brother back. Only you were my little brother, and I could boss *you* around for a change."

His nephew laughed. Dimitrios felt the dark clouds begin to disperse.

"I'd like to climb the peak with you, Leon."

"I'd love it," his nephew responded emotionally.

"Good. Then we'll plan it after I get back from my honeymoon."

"Honeymoon?"

"Yes." Dimitrios realized that nothing less than marriage would satisfy him. "I'm going to take a long one, and I'll need someone to run things in New York while I'm away."

"Are you serious?"

"Of course. Who else would I ask to fill in for me? Maybe by the time I return home, you'll know better if you want to finish college and go into business with me, or live the religious life.

"Personally, I'd like my nephew with me. Any sons or daughters I have won't be able to help me until I'm a much older man."

"Uncle, you're going too fast for me."

That's the point, Leon. I want to fill your head with enough ideas to confuse you.

"I feel breathless these days."

"You're in love with Ms. Hamilton, aren't you."

Dimitrios's eyes closed tightly. "Yes."

"I knew it the moment you told me to take her to the villa with us."

"You have all the right instincts, Leon. That's why you'll make it in business if that's what you choose."

Another long period of quiet followed before his nephew spoke again. "Have you asked her to marry you?"

"As soon as the fair is over."

"I don't pretend to know her, but she must be wonderful because I've never seen you this happy in my life."

"She's a gift, but you're the only person I've told. I'd like to keep it a secret until we're ready to announce our plans."

"I won't say anything, not even to Mother."

"I've always been able to trust you. Thanks again for being willing to stand in for me at the parade. We'll meet at the villa tomorrow before the family dinner. I want to see you in that costume."

"She had it made for you."

"True, but we're blood, so it's the same thing."

"You're sure you're going to be all right?" The concern in his voice spoke volumes.

"Alexandra is better than any nurse. She won't let anything happen to me."

"That's good. Just be careful. I love you, Uncle."

"I love you, too, Leon. More than you know."

He rang off, then sank back against the pillow.

Seeds had been sown. Only time would tell if they'd fallen on fertile ground.

As for the woman lying within touching distance, her days of being known as Ms. Hamilton were almost over.

If it weren't for the fair, he'd snatch her away this very night to somewhere they could lose themselves in each other for days and nights on end. It was going to be a long night.

The next morning after breakfast at the lodge dining room and a quick inspection of the impeccable silk exhibits in Soufli, the flight back to Thessalonica in the helicopter provided its own set of thrills for Alex.

Under Dimitrios's guidance, the pilot flew low over castles and churches dotting the ancient landscape, giving her a history lesson she would always cherish. But when it came in for a landing on top of the Pandakis building, Alex was the one who suddenly felt strange.

Dimitrios got out of his seat, ready to assist her. She undid her seat belt and started to stand up, then weaved in place.

His powerful arms immediately went around her. "What's wrong?" he demanded anxiously.

"Would you believe I'm the one feeling dizzy?"

"You're having a bout of vertigo. It sometimes happens when you're not used to landing above ground. I'll carry you inside."

"No, please!" she cried in a hushed tone. Last night she'd tasted a little bit of heaven. But it was morning now, and everything had gone back to reality. "Just let me hold onto your arm and I'll be fine in a minute."

"Would you prefer to wait here until it subsides?"

"No— I think maybe that's what's wrong. Knowing we're up so high and—"

"Come on. Let's get you inside the building."

She clung to him while he half pulled her along. Part of the time she kept her eyes closed. He helped her down the stairs from the roof to his suite of offices on the top floor.

Being inside helped a lot.

"Better?" he whispered close to her cheek.

"Much." *Just don't touch me anymore.*

"Drink this."

He'd stopped at the water dispenser and put a cup of it to her lips. It tasted good. She drank the whole thing. As she handed it back, their eyes met. His searching gaze revealed a depth of concern that shook her to the foundations.

"Thank you." Her voice trembled.

She felt him take a deep breath. "You're welcome. Your color's come back. Are you ready to go the rest of the way? It's only a few steps further."

"I think I can do it without your help now."

He ignored her comment and assisted her inside his office where his staff waited to be introduced to her.

"This is probably the most embarrassing moment of my life."

He ushered her to the couch where she could sit down. "But think what it's doing for Stavros, who has been under the impression you're superhuman."

Alex chuckled in spite of the situation. Within minutes everyone had taken turns greeting her so cordially, she felt right at home. Stavros showed up last of all with a glass of lemonade for her.

He sat down next to her. "I have a confession to make,

my dear,'' he said in excellent English. ''I've never liked flying in the damn thing.''

''Now he tells me!'' Dimitrios pretended to be upset, but his eyes were smiling. When they did that, he was virtually irresistible to Alex.

She drank half the lemonade before she said, ''I think if I just don't have to land on a roof again, I'll be all right.''

''Good for you,'' Stavros murmured. He looked at Dimitrios. ''You're hovering.''

''He does that on occasion,'' Alex couldn't help adding. Already she liked the older man who'd been with the Pandakis firm for so many years.

Now it was Stavros whose eyes were smiling. ''There's a lot of work waiting for you, Dimitrios. If you want to get busy, I'll show Ms. Hamilton into her office.''

She'd never known anyone who spoke to Dimitrios that way. It showed the measure of affection, even love between the two men who treated each other as equals.

Dimitrios muttered something about his secretaries being partners in crime before he wheeled away and strode toward his private office, taking her heart with him.

After finishing her lemonade, she felt restored and was able to get up and follow Stavros without problem. The fabulous office that would be her headquarters during the fair was obviously someone else's inner sanctum. He didn't tell her which of the Pandakis cousins had been asked to make the sacrifice.

For the next hour they got down to business. Toward the end of their meeting, she acted on a suggestion Dimitrios had made in regard to Stavros.

''Before I leave, can I be frank with you?''

"Of course."

"I'm not much of a people person. I would prefer to work behind the scenes from here to make sure every event goes off as planned. You're the mainstay of the corporation, and the only one who can handle the VIPs flying in for the fair. Would you take over in that department? Please?"

He looked surprised. "If that's what you wish."

"It is. To be honest, if I thought I had to entertain foreign dignitaries, I'd probably have a nervous breakdown."

"Dimitrios told me you're not the type to fall apart on him."

"I have to retain a few secrets to stay in with the boss."

The older man's hearty laugh delighted her.

"If I'd known this was going to be a party, I wouldn't have left."

At the sound of Dimitrios's vibrant voice, Alex got up from the desk. Stavros remained in his swivel chair, eyeing her employer in amusement.

"Ms. Hamilton and I have been sorting things out. She's afraid for me to tamper with her work agenda, so it looks like I'm going to be the fair's goodwill ambassador."

"Whatever makes the two of you happy. Now I'm afraid it's getting late. We have to go, Alexandra."

She turned to Stavros. "I'll see you later then. Thank you for everything."

"It's been my pleasure."

Dimitrios cupped her elbow and ushered her out to the elevator. On their ride down to the lobby he seemed to be staring into her soul.

"Did you know that Stavros rarely laughs like that? You made him a happy man. For that, you're going to get a reward."

She shook her head. "Please. No more bonuses."

"Actually I had something else in mind," he said in a quiet voice. "When the fair is over, you'll find out what it is."

Alex didn't want gifts from Dimitrios. What she did want was still out of reach. Last night had to have been an aberration. Right now she had to keep reminding herself that the only reason he kept a hold was because she'd been dizzy earlier.

He didn't let go until he'd helped her climb in the back of the limousine waiting for them.

"Oh—my suitcase!"

"It's in the trunk with my backpack."

Dimitrios went around to his side of the car. After he issued instructions to the driver, they were off.

"Isn't the hotel the other way?" Alexandra cried as the limo made an unexpected right turn.

He nodded. "Yes. However, we still have work to do after dinner. There's no time to ferry you back and forth. Now that I know Michael and his friends can entertain themselves, it only makes sense you stay at the villa. As for your friend Yanni, he and his girlfriend might as well use the other bedroom in your suite, which is going to waste."

After a pregnant pause, "How long do you expect the party to last?"

"I have no idea. Does it matter? You're my guest. Naturally you'll be attending the dinner with me."

"But I'm not family."

Dimitrios cursed beneath his breath. "You must have

a poor opinion of me if you think I would leave you on your own! Everyone in the family is anxious to meet the woman who has managed to bring back the splendor of Thessalonica to a world that is looking on in fascination.''

She bowed her head. ''Thank you for the compliment, but as usual, you exaggerate my part in things.'' He heard a deep sigh. ''Should I dress up for dinner, or will one of my suits be all right?''

''Whatever makes you the most comfortable.''

''Maybe I should ask your sister-in-law. She'll have definite ideas.''

''It's not up to Ananke to decide.''

''Isn't she the hostess?''

''No. We'll be eating at Uncle Spiros's villa.''

''I thought he'd passed away.'' Her voice trailed.

''He did. After his death, his son Pantelis moved in with his family. You'll like his wife, Estelle. She doesn't fuss about things that aren't important.''

Another long silence ensued. He glanced at her. ''What's going on in that mind of yours to put such a fierce expression on your face?''

''It may surprise you to know that even nondescript secretaries want to look their best when the occasion demands.''

''In *my* employ you've never presented a less than perfect picture,'' he bit out in frustration. ''If you thought I implied otherwise, you'd be wrong.''

He could feel her pulling away from him. Nothing was the same since they'd left Dadia.

When Nicholas appeared, Dimitrios asked him to bring in their luggage, then he grasped Alex's elbow to escort her through the villa. She seemed in a great hurry to reach the guest bedroom. After what had transpired in the last twenty-four hours, he rebelled at the idea of their being separated for any reason.

"Be ready to leave in an hour."

She nodded, then started to shut the door.

"Alexandra—"

"Yes?" she said, sounding as breathless as he felt. "Is there something you forgot to tell me? Something you want me to do?"

There was so much he wanted from her, he wasn't able to think with any coherence. "It can wait."

With that oblique comment, he turned and strode toward his suite. Alex shut the door, then leaned upon it. She couldn't understand what had come over him. Maybe it had to do with this house that once upon a time contained the family he'd lost. He always seemed happier away from it.

Last night when he'd held out his hands for her to dance, he'd been a totally different person. Alex had never known such ecstasy as those moments in his powerful arms with the wine and the music feeding the flame of her desire.

Again she was struck by the fact that he'd always accepted her just the way she was. She loved him for it. But right now he sounded so upset. What had she said?

A shiver passed through her body. There'd only been a few times at the office when she'd seen him truly angry. The last thing she'd ever want was to be his target, even if it were deserved.

Once again Alex found herself wishing she dared to be her real self for tonight. If it weren't for the likelihood of Giorgio being at the party, Alex was tempted to end the charade for good.

A knock on the door made her jump. She thought it was Dimitrios, that he'd changed his mind and had come back to ask a favor of her. When she opened it, she discovered Nicholas standing there with her suitcase. He placed it inside the room.

Though she needed it to get ready, she felt a bitter disappointment that it wasn't Dimitrios. She quickly thanked the other man, then shut the door after him.

Almost to the bathroom, tears streamed down her face. Too much had transpired in the last twenty-four hours to contain her emotions any longer. She needed a release.

Half an hour later, she padded over to the suitcase with a towel wrapped around her and pulled out the only dressy outfit she'd brought from New York.

When Michael had planned her wardrobe, they'd laughed over the choices he'd come up with. But Alex wasn't laughing now. She lifted the boxy, drab, gray three-piece suit to her gaze. The wrinkle-proof affair felt like stiff taffeta. Her eyes studied the beading on the collar and cuffs.

It was hideous. She could hardly bare to put it on, but she had no choice.

One glance in the mirror and she was equally repulsed by her dyed brown hair, which she wore in an eternal twist pulled back from an unimaginative center part. Alex's mother wasn't the only person who didn't know what she looked like these days.

It astounded her that Dimitrios didn't appear to mind being seen with her.

"Alexandra?" His peremptory voice was followed by a rap on the door.

"I'm ready."

She slipped into her black matron shoes once more,

then reached for the door handle. If he said one word about how nice she looked…

But at her first glimpse of the tall, virile male dressed in a long-sleeved black silk shirt teamed with black trousers, she forgot all about the ghastly picture she presented.

"Leon and his mother are waiting for us in the car. They're both under the impression that I'm still too unsteady to mount a horse, so play along with me while I hang onto you for support. Shall we go?"

Once again he ushered her down the hall with his arm around her shoulders. The familiar smell of the soap he'd used in the shower assailed her again. He was clean-shaven tonight. Dimitrios had to be the most gorgeous man alive. How comical she must look standing next to him!

The strange glance Ananke flashed her when they got in the back of the limousine verified Alex's opinion of herself. But Leon's eyes were kind as they rested on her.

"Good evening, Ms. Hamilton."

"I'm so glad to see you again, Leon. Since the other day I've wanted to apologize to you for anything I said that upset you."

He shook his head. "No, no. I was the idiot. We don't need to talk about it again." Just then he sounded and acted very much like Dimitrios.

His mother chose that moment to say something to her brother-in-law.

"Speak English, Ananke."

"It's my opinion you should stay home from the party, Dimitrios. You should never have left your bed yesterday."

"I agree with you, Mrs. Pandakis," Alex inserted.

"Considering the fact that we still have work to do this evening after dinner, I don't think he should stay long. Not when he's still feeling light-headed."

"Then it's settled," his nephew declared with surprising finality. "We will eat quickly and leave."

"Thank you all for deciding for me."

Dimitrios's wry comment prompted Alex to mutter, "Someone has to."

"I'll make it a short night on one condition."

"What's that?" Ananke asked the question foremost on Alex's mind.

"After Ms. Hamilton went to all the trouble of having a costume made for me, I want the family to see Leon model it before he wears it in the parade tomorrow."

"I'd be happy to do that, Uncle, but it's too late now. We'll be at the villa in a moment."

Alex darted her host a sideward glance and caught a gleam in his eye. "As it happens, I asked Nicholas to put it in the trunk."

Leon wouldn't be able to wiggle out of it now.

Pleased to see Dimitrios's tactics working where his nephew was concerned, Alex turned her head and looked out the window.

They'd been passing through another beautiful residential area of the city. As they turned into a private drive lined with cars, she caught sight of a pastel villa built along neoclassical lines. It looked even larger and more imposing than the one they'd just come from.

Mrs. Landau had once confided to Alex that even if Spiros headed the Pandakis family and had four sons to help run the company, his brother's son, Dimitrios, was the driving force.

True to her prediction, after Spiros's death there really

wasn't a transfer of power because Dimitrios was already the natural leader to whom the entire family and business magnates deferred.

It would be interesting to see if, after all Dimitrios had done to let Leon make his own decisions about life, his nephew ended up showing the same spark of business genius as his illustrious uncle. Stranger things had happened.

For Ananke's sake, Alex hoped her son would marry and have children. The other woman was suffering. Her husband had been dead too many years for her to be actively grieving. Alex surmised that her pain stemmed from another source. She also had the impression Leon wasn't the sole cause of it.

"We've arrived," Dimitrios whispered against her ear. She knew it was accidental, but his lips grazed her lobe. His touch sent tiny ripples of delight through her system.

"Leon?" he called to his nephew. "I'll help your mother inside while you take the garment bag and get ready."

"Yes, Uncle."

Alex struggled not to smile. Leon wasn't used to Dimitrios making demands, but as far as she was concerned, it was exactly what he needed.

Within minutes both Alex and Ananke flanked Dimitrios as they made their way around the side of the villa to a terrace where a large crowd was gathered. Alex counted at least thirty beautifully dressed family members.

Spiros's sons were all married with children, some of whom looked to be in their teens. Coupled with staff loading food on the tables placed around the ornate gardens, it made an impressive sight.

"Dimitrios!" someone cried in delight.

"Don't move from my side," he cautioned her.

CHAPTER EIGHT

ALEX was only too happy to oblige her host. Before he'd spoken, she'd spotted Giorgio Pandakis among the crowd. He was shorter than his brothers and had put on weight since the frightening experience trying to fend him off outside the silk museum.

Back then she'd found him the least attractive of the Pandakis men. The same held true tonight. She shuddered.

Dimitrios eyed her curiously. "Are you cold?" He noticed everything.

"No. I thought I saw a bug coming for me," she lied.

His quick smile made her breath catch. "If you did, it was a moth. We get them this time of year. It won't hurt you."

She looked away as everyone came rushing toward them speaking Greek so fast and furiously Alex could only catch certain words or phrases. Her host was the obvious favorite, especially with the little children who grabbed hold of his legs wanting him to pick them up.

But Ananke put a halt to that and led him to a chair at one of the tables where she sat down next to him. Alex followed and took her place at his other side.

Besieged by questions she knew concerned his accident, Dimitrios patiently answered each one while they ate. After being introduced to his cousins Pantelis and Takis, she was glad they spoke to him and Ananke. Alex was able to stay in the background.

She was halfway through her meal when she heard someone cry out. This time the attention turned away from Dimitrios because Leon had walked out on the terrace.

Alex let out a quiet gasp because the costume fit him perfectly. With the flowing ruby cape and scepter, he looked like the saint on the icon come to life. All the noise quieted down as the family stared at him in fascination.

Alex saw Dimitrios smile at his nephew. Whatever he said to him in Greek caused Leon to smile back with real affection.

"Attention everyone," her host switched to English. "Tomorrow Leon will be taking my place in the parade. Thanks to the genius of my secretary, Ms. Hamilton, who planned the entire trade fair and had this costume made, I can see that Leon will do the Pandakis clan proud."

Everyone clapped and begged him to walk around so they could get a good look. Alex had the distinct impression his nephew was loving all the attention. He really did look wonderful and stayed in costume throughout the duration of the dinner.

Little by little, different family members came over to the table to make her acquaintance. One of the wives said in excellent English, "How did you ever think of such a clever costume?"

Guilt made the heat rush to Alex's cheeks. "Actually it was very simple. Saint Dimitrios is a well-known figure in history, and my employer happened to bear his name."

Dimitrios cocked his head. "So if my name had been Hades, you would have immediately produced a costume for me?"

His comment was so unexpected, Alex burst into laughter, forgetting where she was. "Except for the god of the underworld, I've never heard of anyone being named Hades."

"I've never heard you laugh like that before," he said in a husky aside. "You should do it more often."

Her heart ached to take his comment personally, but she knew he was only trying to help her feel comfortable among a crowd of strangers.

By now another of his dark-haired cousins had approached their table, obviously interested in the byplay that made her and Dimitrios the center of attention instead of Leon.

"Ms. Hamilton? Meet Vaso, my cousin and good friend."

Vaso smiled and shook her hand. "It's a pleasure to be introduced to you at last. You and Dimitrios should have been at the dinner I attended last night. The prime minister expressed disappointment that he wasn't able to compliment the American woman who put this spectacular trade fair together. Those were his exact words."

"Thank you," she murmured.

Vaso gave Dimitrios a playful punch on the shoulder. "He says he might steal her away from you to work on his trade council in the future. Watch out, cousin."

Dimitrios smiled at her with his eyes. It would have been one of the most exciting moments of her life if she hadn't seen Giorgio moving toward them at the same time Vaso walked away.

Since her arrival in Greece she'd been afraid of the time when she would have to come face to face with him. Now that time was here, and there was no place to run.

"Good evening, Dimitrios. Sorry to hear you're still not completely recovered from your mishap."

"Thank you, Giorgio. May I present my secretary who has made me the envy of the prime minister himself. Ms. Hamilton, allow me to present my cousin Giorgio."

"How do you do," she said without meeting his gaze.

He kissed the back of her hand, but didn't immediately relinquish it. She couldn't stand for a man to do that and was reminded of the time he'd grabbed hold of her, not letting go until Dimitrios had pulled him off her. It brought back the terror of that night with a clarity that made her break out in a cold sweat.

She removed her hand, uncaring if it offended him.

Undaunted, his cousin remained in place. "That is a famous American name."

"You're right, Giorgio. As it happens, Alexandra was named after her great-great-great-grandfather Alexander Hamilton, the renowned American politician who started the national bank and became the first United States Secretary of the Treasury."

"Ah. That explains your phenomenal rise in the Pandakis Corporation. With the trade fair to your credit, you've made yourself indispensable to my cousin. Congratulations."

Alex didn't miss the flash of hostility in Dimitrios's eyes before Giorgio excused himself.

Her heart hammered in her ears. "How did you know about my ancestry?"

"If you recall, Mrs. Landau was a genealogy buff. One day she happened to mention it to me."

"She was a regular treasure trove of knowledge," Alex muttered in a sarcastic tone to cover her relief at the explanation.

For a minute she thought he had made the connection to her grandfather who'd hosted the silk seminar nine years ago. That would have meant telling Dimitrios the whole truth tonight. Thank heaven she could wait until she wrote her letter of resignation before unburdening herself.

"Mrs. Landau had great faith in you. Her praise of your work was the only reason you became my private secretary after her passing."

She ought to have been pleased Mrs. Landau had championed her, but somehow she wasn't. Sometimes it was better not to know the truth.

"Forget what Giorgio said," The light had gone from Dimitrios's eyes as if it had never been. "Unfortunately he has a propensity for making mischief. Since I can see he's put you off your dessert, we'll leave now."

Alex needed no urging to get as far away from Giorgio as possible. Together they stood up from the table.

Ananke followed suit. "I'll find Leon and meet you both at the car."

As she hurried away, Dimitrios slanted his gaze toward Alex. "For my nephew's sake, be prepared to steady me, even after we get home. I don't want him to think he can squeeze out of this now."

"I don't think he wants to," she whispered. "From where I was sitting, your mantle appeared to feel good on his shoulders."

"I hope you're right."

Within a few minutes they were ensconced in the limo. Alex sat back to watch the scenery while the three of them conversed in Greek. Leon chatted nonstop with a continual smile on his attractive face. It was a very good sign. Even Ananke's spirits seemed to have picked up a little.

Almost to the villa, Alex's cell phone rang. As she pulled it out of her purse and clicked on, a grimace suddenly marred Dimitrios's features.

"Hello?"

"You're a difficult one to get hold of these days."

"Michael! Are you all having a good time?"

"Of course, but we haven't seen you yet. Your friend Yanni and his girlfriend arrived a few minutes ago."

"Yanni's there now?"

"Yes. Why don't you come over to the hotel for a while and prove to us you're not a figment of our imagination. I want to hear the lowdown. That is, if your lord and master will let you go."

She bit her lip. "I—I don't think I can tonight," she murmured, not able to explain while Dimitrios was aware of every breath she took. Giorgio had changed the tenor of the evening for both of them.

"It's obvious you can't talk right now so call us later, darling."

The line went dead.

She put the phone back in her purse, pretending that she had no idea Dimitrios had been listening.

When the limo pulled up in front of the villa, Leon helped his mother out, then opened the door for his uncle before he took Ananke inside.

Alex got out and hurried around to offer Dimitrios her support, but he didn't make a move to enter the foyer. Instead he leveled his black gaze on her.

"I'm sorry if you wanted to be with your friends tonight, but your presence here will convince my nephew I'm still not back to normal."

"I realize that."

He checked his watch. "It's only ten to ten. Why don't you invite them over here for a swim."

"Tonight?" she cried in shock.

"Yes. The evening is warm. Perhaps it will prove I'm not quite the ogre they've imagined."

She blushed, recalling Michael's last comment. "They don't think any such thing!"

One corner of his mouth lifted, making him overwhelmingly attractive. "That's nice to hear. In that case I'll tell Kristofor to pick them up while you make the call."

"It's very kind of you. You have no idea how thrilled they'll be to meet you in person. To be a guest in your villa will make the whole trip for them."

"Good. I'm glad we have that settled. Leon liked your friend Michael. He'll probably want to join us."

She hesitated. "I—I don't swim." She hated telling lies. She hoped this would be the last one.

"No problem. My nephew will find it suspect if he discovers me doing laps in the pool when I'm supposed to be recuperating. You and I can lounge in the deck chairs and do some last-minute business while we watch them."

In the next breath she could hear him giving directions to Kristofor. So in love with Dimitrios she didn't know where to go with her feelings, Alex did the only thing she could do and pulled out her cell phone to call the hotel. Michael was about to get the surprise of his life!

"I've never seen you looking lovelier, Alexandra. With that shade of brown hair, gray is definitely *your* color," Michael quipped sotto voce forty-five minutes later. How he could keep a straight face was beyond Alex, who gave him a hug.

"You're wicked, you know that?"

"Of course." He winked. "Where's the great Kyrie?"

"By the pool."

"This place is a living museum. How would it be…"

"Heavenly," she answered in a tremulous voice.

"I can see that. You'd better be careful or he's going to see it, too, if he hasn't already."

"I know," she murmured, suitably chastened.

They followed Leon, who offered to give them a tour of the ground floor of the villa before their swim.

It pleased Alex that her friends got along so well with Dimitrios's nephew. The three of them had performed in many Greek plays and shared his love of the theater.

Yanni loved contemporary theater. He took in every New York play possible. Between the six of them, they kept up a lively discussion until Leon led them to the rectangular pool at the back of the villa. There the Grecian garden setting took everyone's breath.

But Alex had eyes only for Dimitrios who got to his feet when he saw them. Still in his black shirt and trousers, he was so devastatingly handsome it hurt to look at him.

He couldn't have been more gracious. His arresting personality made an impact on everyone, but especially on Michael, who during a stolen moment arched an eyebrow as if to say, *Your obsession is no longer a mystery.*

Leon showed them where to change. In a few minutes he'd jumped in the deep end of the pool with them. Before long he had them competing in a frantic game of water polo.

Dimitrios's nephew possessed the same kind of athletic ability as his uncle and could outplay the lot of them. As the night wore on, Alex realized she wasn't the only person who noticed what a fine specimen Leon was.

The longer the others played, the more obvious it became that Yanni's redheaded Greek girlfriend found Leon attractive. To Alex's chagrin, it appeared Leon returned the compliment. Unfortunately that wasn't supposed to have happened. Yanni was no longer smiling.

Alarmed by the unexpected situation, Alex put down the notes she'd been going over with Dimitrios. Her troubled eyes met the speculation in his. Nothing escaped his notice.

"Are Yanni and Merlina engaged?" He'd asked the question in a low voice that no one else could have heard.

She took a deep breath. "No. He has another girlfriend in New York."

"Do you want me to do something about it?"

Alex knew what he meant. It was a loaded question.

She liked Yanni and didn't want to see him hurt. It would be hard to compete with all this and Leon, a good-looking man who was showing all the charm and promise of the breathtaking male sitting next to her.

On the other hand...

"It might not hurt for Leon to realize he's the object of female admiration right now. Merlina's a beautiful girl. If her interest in him can add to his confusion about where he wants to go with his life, it could be a good thing."

"You're reading my mind again. So what about your friend Yanni?"

She hunched her shoulders. "He says he isn't looking for anything permanent yet. Maybe a little healthy competition is what he needs. Someday he'll have to make an honest woman out of one of his girlfriends.''

He studied her briefly. ''Until I met you, I didn't think there was such a thing as an honest woman.''

His cynical comment, delivered without a trace of levity, swept the foundation out from under her. She could hear her mother's warning.

You've just told me he's an honorable man when it comes to business. Men like that expect honor in return. Mark my words, Alexandra. Every minute you're in his employ, you're playing with fire.

Groaning inwardly, she got up from the lounger with her notes. ''I can't thank you enough for opening up your beautiful home and making my friends feel welcome. But it's getting late, and I have to be down by the grandstand early in the morning to help coordinate everything for the parade. I'll tell Michael they have to leave.''

To her surprise, he rose to his feet. ''They're having a good time. Let's not interrupt them. Leon will take care of everything.''

He grasped her upper arm as if he really needed help. They left the pool area without anyone noticing. On their way through the villa she asked him where he planned to be during the parade.

''I'll drop Ananke off at the grandstand, then go to my office and watch the proceedings on television. As soon as Leon has given his speech, I'll meet you at the launch where we'll be taken out to the Cleopatra barge for lunch with Stavros and some visiting dignitaries.''

Outside her room she finally dared to look up at him. ''I hope the fair is going to be a success. I want things to be perfect for you.''

"They already are. Good night, Alexandra. Sleep well."

"You, too," she said before closing the door.

But the moment she found herself alone in the room, she realized she'd reached a point of no return with Dimitrios. Tonight he'd told her she was the only honest woman he knew. Alex loved him too much to let him go on believing something that wasn't true. She had to go to him right now and make a full confession, otherwise she wouldn't be able to live with herself another second. If he fired her on the spot, then it was only what she deserved.

Without wasting any time, she left her room. Hoping no one would see her, she hurried to his door. Silence followed her knock. Maybe he was in the shower. She didn't know what to think.

"Dimitrios?" she called urgently and knocked again.

Suddenly the door opened.

He'd answered it with his shirt partially unbuttoned. One look at the rapid rise and fall of his well-defined chest with its dusting of dark hair and her mouth went dry.

She lifted her eyes to his, but that was a mistake. They were veiled, making it impossible to tell if he was annoyed at the interruption.

He leaned one hand against the doorjamb. "Was there some last-minute decision concerning the parade you needed to talk to me about?"

His deep male voice played havoc with her senses. She could smell alcohol on his breath. Alex had never caught him drinking alone. There had to be a reason for such uncharacteristic behavior.

She rubbed her damp palms nervously against her taffeta-covered hips. "No— What I wanted to talk about doesn't have anything to do with the fair. But obviously I waited too long to disturb you. Forgive me."

He must have sensed her intentions because he grasped her forearm before she could walk away. "There's nothing to forgive. Come in, Alexandra. I was just having a nightcap to help me sleep."

"You must be more worried about your nephew than you've been letting on."

His eyes narrowed on her mouth, making her insides quiver. "That and other things," came the vague explanation. He pushed the door closed behind her. Her gaze flitted to the table where she saw a small half-empty glass.

"I'd offer you a drink, but something tells me you wouldn't like the flavor of retsina. If this is going to take a while, come all the way in and sit down."

She couldn't back down and followed him to the table where she did his bidding. "Dimitrios—"

"That's a good beginning. For some reason I haven't figured out yet, you seem to have trouble saying it."

"B-because first names blur the lines between a worker and an employer."

"Surely by now I mean a little more to you than that."

"Yes. We've become good friends." Her heart was pounding so outrageously, she squirmed on the chair. "I feel I could tell you anything."

"Is that why you're here?"

"Yes." She moistened her dry lips nervously. "Tonight you made a statement about my being the only honest woman you'd ever met."

"I never say anything I don't mean."

"Then you need to know I haven't been completely honest with you about something very important."

His eyes held a strange glitter. "It must be, for you to come knocking at my door. Go on. I'm listening."

"T-this has to do with an experience that happened to me a long time ago."

"With a man?" he demanded quietly.

"Yes."

She felt his stillness before hearing his sharp intake of breath. "Were you raped?"

"Almost," she answered shakily. "But another man came along in time to save me."

"Thank God," sounded the emotional response. "How old were you when it happened?"

"Sixteen."

"*Now* I understand why you wear clothes that intentionally hide your body."

Her eyes closed tightly for a moment. He was so close, yet so far from the mark.

"I hope the man who saved you beat him to a bloody pulp before turning him in to the police."

"H-he knocked him unconscious, and I loved him for it," she said on a half-sob. "In fact I've loved him ever since. Dimitrios, that man—"

But Alex was prevented from finishing her confession because the door suddenly flew open.

She turned in the chair as Leon swept into the room. He slowed to a stop when he saw her.

"Ms. Hamilton—I didn't realize you were in here. I knocked." His gaze darted to Dimitrios. "Are you feeling worse?"

"That's what I came in to ask him," she interjected

before Dimitrios could say anything. "But he insists he's fine and felt like having a drink before going to bed."

"You really shouldn't, Uncle. Not until you're completely out of the woods."

"Perhaps you're right," Dimitrios muttered. "What can I do for you, Leon?"

"I was hoping if you weren't too tired, I could go over my speech with you. Tomorrow morning will be too late. I don't want to shame you in front of the whole world."

Alex shook her head. "You couldn't possibly do that, Leon."

Alex got up from the chair and raised herself on tiptoe to whisper in his ear. "At least a half year ago Mrs. Landau confided that your uncle wanted you to open the trade fair. He should have acted on those feelings sooner, but he's never wanted to force you into doing things. His uncle Spiros did enough strong-arming to last a lifetime."

Leon's eyes grew suspiciously bright. "Thanks for telling me," he whispered back.

"You're welcome."

"I resent being treated as if I'm not in the room," Dimitrios bellowed.

"You're supposed to be resting," she teased with more daring than usual.

Her confession would have to wait a little while longer.

She'd go to her room and leave the door ajar. As soon as Leon passed by, she'd return to Dimitrios and finish what she'd started.

"Before I say good-night, I'd like to thank you for being so nice to my friends, Leon. They loved the tour of the villa. I've known them for years and could tell they had the time of their lives tonight.''

He grinned. ''I had a good time, too. In fact they asked me to go back to the hotel to party with them. But this speech has made it impossible. I asked Kristofor to drive them home. Tomorrow we're all going to meet after the parade and enjoy the fair together. I'm going to bring some girls I know to come with us.''

''The guys will love it. Greek women are as gorgeous as the men.''

''Did you hear that, Uncle?'' Leon threw his head back and laughed exactly as she'd seen Dimitrios do on their trip.

Alex smiled. ''Go ahead and mock me all you want, but it's true. By the way, you looked pretty terrific in that costume. Merlina's eyes are going to pop right out when she sees you in the parade tomorrow.''

A ruddy color stained his cheeks. ''You think?''

''I *know*. All's fair in love and war,'' she teased. ''Good luck tomorrow, but your uncle told me you won't need it.'' She kissed his jaw.

''Good night, Kyrie Pandakis.''

''Don't I get one of those too?''

She ignored Dimitrios's comment and slipped out of the room.

Under the circumstances, she was thankful that as long as Leon had been determined to see his uncle tonight, he'd come in before she'd had the chance to blurt everything out.

There was no miracle gauge to calculate how angry Dimitrios was going to be when he learned the truth. Since Leon had needed his uncle tonight, it was best that she'd left Dimitrios in a somewhat mellow mood.

Upon reaching her room, she left the door open a few inches, then turned out the lights. She hoped Leon wouldn't stay too long.

Alex lay down on her side across the bed so she could keep an eye on the hallway. She decided not to change. It would require all the confidence she could summon to face Dimitrios.

Whatever the consequences, her mother would be overjoyed when Alex phoned to report that the truth was out at last. In Alex's heart of hearts, she would be relieved, too. But it meant never seeing Dimitrios again.

Zeus would have to return to his immortal state as the mythological god in her art history book. A book she would never open again.

She rested her head on her arm as hot tears trickled out of the corners of her eyes.

CHAPTER NINE

"So what do you think, Uncle?"

Dimitrios got up off the bed to face his nephew. "Would you believe me if I told you?"

Leon answered yes.

He eyed his brother's boy who'd become a man over the last year. Dimitrios didn't know the exact moment the transformation had occurred, but he liked what he saw very much.

"It's a masterpiece of fresh ideas, optimism and surprising faith in mankind. Many people feel the world has already seen its golden days. You have a vision that sees golden days to come." He put a hand on his shoulder. "I'm proud to be related to you."

Leon had to clear his throat. "I feel the same way about you. Thank you," he muttered before hugging Dimitrios hard.

"I'm sorry to have walked in on you and Alexandra like that. I had no idea."

Dimitrios patted him one more time, then stepped back. "She and I have the rest of the night."

"Then I'm going to get out of here now. When I wave from my horse tomorrow, I'll be waving to you and Mother."

"She'll be in tears the entire time she's in the grandstand. I'm going to have it taped at the office so she can watch her son's triumphant entry into Thessalonica whenever she gets lonely for you."

Leon's eyes slid away.

Dimitrios didn't know whether to take that as a sign that his nephew had definitely made up his mind. But now wasn't the time to solve all the riddles.

The woman next door had been on the verge of telling him something vital when they'd been interrupted. He had the awful premonition she was planning to leave his employ to marry the man who'd saved her from being violated.

Dimitrios couldn't accept that.

Whatever she felt for her rescuer was hero-worship, gratitude. It had nothing to do with the kind of intimacy Dimitrios had enjoyed with her these past few days. Theirs was that rare bonding of flesh and spirit. A trust that couldn't be broken. *A love to die for.*

Leonides hadn't been allowed to live long enough to find what Dimitrios had found.

Aching to express his feelings, he left the room after Leon disappeared and walked next door to Alexandra's room.

To his surprise, her door was ajar. He pushed it open a little more. There was enough light from the hall to see her lying on the bed, still dressed in what she'd been wearing earlier. She had to have been exhausted to do that.

He listened to her breathing. She was in a deep sleep.

After everything she'd done to make the trade fair run to perfection, it would be criminal of him to waken her now.

Afraid to stand there for fear he'd join her on that bed, he went to his room for a cold shower. As he turned on the spray, he vowed that this was the last night he was going to lie in his bed alone writhing with unassuaged longings.

Eight hours later, a beaming Stavros tossed half a dozen newspapers on the table in front of Dimitrios while he sat in front of the television waiting for the parade coverage to start.

"In Japanese, English or Greek, it's the same story on the front page of every major journal." He shook his head. "Ms. Hamilton is a veritable genius. Trust her to give the newspapers a quote from the chronicler of the twelfth-century fair to begin the article."

It pleased him that Stavros held the future Mrs. Pandakis in such high regard. He reached for the Athenian News and began reading.

The Demetria is a festival, the most important fair held in Macedonia. Not only do the natives flock together to it in great numbers, but they come from all lands and every race.

Dimitrios put the paper down and cleared his throat. "You're right, Stavros. She's recreated something people aren't going to forget."

"She has the attention of the prime minister."

"So Vaso told me."

"Do you think she would leave you to take another position?"

"I hope not. As soon as the fair is over I'm asking her to marry me."

When Stavros didn't say anything, Dimitrios turned his head to glance at his mentor, who'd just pulled a handkerchief out of his pocket.

He frowned. "Are you all right?"

"Yes, yes. Of course."

"Then why aren't you saying anything?"

"I think I'm overcome."

Dimitrios smiled to himself. "I didn't know that was possible."

"Congratulations, my boy."

"Keep it under your hat."

"Since when have we ever announced a deal until it was all sewn up?"

"All sewn up is the operative phrase, Stavros. Last night I found out she thinks she's in love with someone else."

"Knowing you as I do, you'll get around that little problem. Oh—the coverage is beginning." Stavros sat down on the couch next to him to watch.

Dimitrios felt gooseflesh as trumpets sounded and he saw his nephew lead a contingent of soldiers on horseback through the throng of people lining the packed streets under a sunny sky. They shouted and waved to him in celebration.

Leon sat tall in the saddle, his red cape flowing, the gold scepter held high in his right hand. Dimitrios's eyes blurred.

But inevitably his thoughts wandered to Alexandra, who'd slipped away from the villa earlier in the morning before he could catch her.

If she'd never come to work for him, there would be no trade fair in Thessalonica. Without her there'd be no costume made expressly for him. He'd find no joy in getting up to meet the day because she wouldn't be a part of it. The thought of life without her was too unfathomable to contemplate.

Stavros pulled out his handkerchief again. "If Leon decides for the ministry, he definitely looks the part."

"Yes."

"I can only hope that wherever your brother is, he's looking on to see what a fine son he has. Ananke will be the proudest mother in all Thessalonica today."

For the next two hours they stayed glued to the set watching the tumbling acts, banners, dancers and floats from every province in Greece. Enchanted, Dimitrios was bursting with pride by the time his nephew delivered his speech to the crowd.

When he'd finished, the prime minister stepped forward. He bid Leon kneel so he could place a garland of laurel leaves on his head. The throng roared their approval.

Stavros's voice sounded gruff when he said, "I don't think that was in the original script."

"A very nice gesture from the prime minister."

"He asked you to get the job done. Your bride-to-be answered him a hundredfold."

"I'm going to find her, Stavros. We'll meet you on board the barge in an hour."

Except that plans had a way of changing.

After Dimitrios had been pacing in front of the launch at the pier for half an hour, Alexandra phoned to say something had come up to do with a group of translators for the fair. Their bus from the university had broken down en route to a designated location. She needed to go back to the office arrange other transportation for them and wouldn't be able to join him for lunch.

Dimitrios's degree of disappointment was so severe, he realized he couldn't go on this way any longer. With his emotions in utter chaos, he made his own excuses regarding the lunch, then called for his driver to take him to the office. He'd reached the point that if he couldn't be with Alexandra, nothing else interested him.

Alex spotted Dimitrios's well-honed frame as he swept through the reception area of the suite. The place resembled a florist's shop at the moment. Several hundred offerings of flowers sat on desks, lined corridors and decorated file cabinets.

The outpouring from business associates and government officials was a touching tribute to Dimitrios, but he seemed oblivious as he headed straight for her office.

Her heart leaped at the sight of him. He was dressed in a dove-gray silk suit and dazzling white shirt, but lines had darkened his handsome face, making him appear remote.

"What's wrong?" she asked the second he stepped over the threshold.

"Remind me to tell you when we're alone. Now that Leon's part in the fair is over, we won't have to worry about being interrupted again."

If she didn't have a confession to make tonight, his words would have brought her the greatest joy imaginable.

"Your nephew was magnificent today."

"I thought so, too," he murmured.

"It's been very exciting to hear all the favorable compliments about the parade and the part he played."

He captured her gaze. "The moment you presented me the drawing of Thessalonica during the twelfth-century fair, there was never any doubt in my mind it would be a success."

This had been her hope and dream for Dimitrios. She could be thankful for that much.

"The prime minister sent that huge spray of flowers over in the corner."

Dimitrios stood behind her while she opened the card

to show him. When his body brushed against hers, she almost fainted from the sensation.

"How do I thank him?"

"Would you like to accept a position on his trade commission? That's what he's angling for."

And remain in Greece so close to you, knowing I can never be with you again?

"I'm very honored, but no."

"In that case you could pen him a personal note. I'll see that it's attached to an acknowledgment from the corporation. We'll be sending one to every donor. He'll enjoy that."

"I'll write it before I leave the office today. Shall we send the flowers to the hospitals?"

He nodded. "The staff will take care of it."

"Then I'd better get busy answering e-mails."

"Uncle?"

Alex was getting used to the sound of Leon's voice.

She looked over her shoulder in time see Dimitrios hug his nephew. Then it was her turn to congratulate him.

To her surprise, he wasn't alone. Michael and his friends had trailed in after him, but there was no sign of Yanni or Merlina.

"We've had a change in plans," Leon began without preamble. "If it's all right with you, I'm taking the guys to Mount Athos. We'll be back tomorrow evening to take in a play. They're putting on *Phaedra*."

To Dimitrios's credit, he didn't reveal his emotions. It was Alex who had to bite her tongue not to say anything. Her disappointment in his nephew's decision caused her spirits to plunge to new depths.

"I'm fine with that," Dimitrios said with enviable calm. "Mount Athos is a unique place."

Michael eyed Alex. "When Leon was telling us about it last night, we asked if we could visit it with him."

"There's just one problem," Leon murmured. "Yanni wants to join us, but Merlina shouldn't be left alone."

Before Leon said anything more, Alex knew what she had to do. It meant her confession would have to be put off a little longer, but it didn't seem she had a choice.

"I'll stay at the hotel with her tonight, Leon. I hear it's a fabulous place and I haven't even stepped inside it yet. Besides, it's the least I can do to repay you for looking after my friends."

"Thank you, Ms. Hamilton."

"I tell you what. I'll phone Yanni right now and tell him to bring Merlina here. She can hang around with me."

Without glancing at Dimitrios, she went over to the desk to make the call. Michael followed.

"Your sacrifice has been noted, but don't look now, darling. Your lord and master is anything but pleased."

"You don't understand, Michael, and there's no time to explain."

"What's going on between you two?" For once Michael had dropped the banter.

"Nothing."

"Then how come you look like your heart is breaking? Why did you let things get this far?"

She blinked hard to fight back the tears. "Because I'm a fool."

"I'm sorry you're in so much pain, Alex. I wish there was something I could do."

"You've been warning me. So has Mom. As soon as I can, I'm telling him the truth. I tried last night, but

Leon interrupted us. I should tell him tonight, but under the circumstances, I'll have to wait a little longer.''

"This is a hell of a time for me to be leaving. When I get back tomorrow we're going to have one of our talks, so plan on it!"

But Michael didn't get back. The other guys were steeped in the arts and wanted to see all of Mount Athos. That meant they had to spend two nights away. Being responsible for Merlina meant Alex was forced to put off her talk with Dimitrios another twenty-four hours.

After months of being with him constantly, the few days without seeing him were the longest, loneliest hours she'd ever known. While he was out covering their VIP lunches and dinners with Stavros, she and Merlina walked all over the city visiting the stalls.

Late Friday afternoon, after the guys had finally returned, Alex took a taxi to the villa. She was going to use her guest room to get ready for a special dinner with some high-ranking Greek dignitaries, which signaled the last night of the fair. On Saturday it would be over.

With one terse message from Dimitrios earlier in the day making it clear she was to attend with him, he clicked off just as abruptly. There was no escaping the fact that tonight he intended getting her alone so they could finish their talk.

Alex dreaded the outcome. But if she could be thankful for just one thing, it was that she'd been given the opportunity to fulfill her professional obligations before everything in her world fell apart.

According to Serilda, who greeted her warmly and brought a cup of tea to her bedroom, no one was home yet, not even Ananke. But she expected Dimitrios home within the hour.

After drinking the hot, sweet liquid, she stepped in the shower to wash her hair. It felt good, but she didn't dare stay in too long. Dimitrios expected her to be ready by six-thirty, which didn't leave her much time to blow dry it and arrange it in a twist. Afterward she'd dress in the ghastly gray suit once more.

Draped in a fluffy towel with her damp hair falling over her shoulders, she padded to the bedroom for fresh underwear. Halfway across the room she froze.

A dark, overweight man dressed in a blue business suit stood against the closed door watching her.

Giorgio.

As his eyes crawled over her body drinking their fill, she tugged the edge of the towel closer around her.

"I was right. You're the sexy little Hamilton girl all grown up."

Terrified because her worst nightmare had become reality, Alex fled to the bathroom. But he'd already lunged for her, preventing her from locking the door against him. He stood over the threshold blocking the exit.

Though he wasn't as tall or powerfully built as Dimitrios, he was still a man. He could best her without problem.

"And you're still the sick little man who'll never measure up to your cousin. Not in an eternity!"

The smile vanished from his face. "You're very clever. I give you credit for that. For the first time in his life, Dimitrios appears to be smitten. That's a major coup considering it's my inscrutable cousin we're talking about."

"Get out!" she raged.

"I don't think so."

"What are you going to do? Finish what you tried the first time before he knocked you unconscious?"

He hunched his shoulders. "If I were drunk, I might be tempted. But I was forced to give up that habit a long time ago. I think what we're going to do is wait for Dimitrios to arrive."

She gritted her teeth. "What is it you want?"

"To see the expression on his face when he realizes the sweet little innocent he once protected so gallantly is none other than the calculating whore who wiggled her ripe body at me one summer night. You were asking for it then.

"Dimitrios didn't believe me, of course. But he will now. Believe me, he will. And then the joke will be on him because he'll realize that even he, the *infallible* one as my father loved to call him, allowed you to slip past his radar."

Dear God. Was everyone in the Pandakis family in pain? The blame for Giorgio's jealousy of Dimitrios could be laid at Spiros's feet. But the damage had been done so long ago, Alex couldn't imagine how any of them would ever heal. It probably wasn't possible.

"You may not believe this, Giorgio, but I had every intention of telling Dimitrios the truth tonight. Why don't you let me get dressed? When he comes, the three of us will sit down and talk this out. No one else will ever have to know."

His bark of angry laughter reverberated against the bathroom walls. "No wonder he was deceived! You have a brain as well as a velvet tongue. You almost got to me just now. No. We'll wait right here where he can see what you've been hiding under those clothes. It was the work of a master."

Tears filled her eyes. "It was the work of a friend who knew how much I loved your cousin and wanted to be close to him."

His head shot forward. "You were a teenager back then. What could you know of love?" he mocked.

Her body shook with pain. "He saved me from you. And he was kind to me. That was the beginning of love." By now the moisture was dripping off her cheeks.

In the silence that followed she heard Dimitrios's rap on the bedroom door. "Alexandra?"

Her heart thudded in her chest.

"Go ahead," Giorgio prodded. "Tell him to come in."

Dimitrios called out a second time.

"Listen to him. So eager for you."

She shook her head. "Don't do this," she begged. "You'll live to regret it."

"My life's been one regret for being born. What's another one? Go on. Tell your beloved he can come in. Or do you want me to invite him in for you?"

Either way she was damned.

Oh, Dimitrios. Forgive me.

"C-come in," she cried in a halting voice.

The door opened and closed. "I hope you're ready. We'll make an appearance at the dinner, then I've planned a surprise for you."

Giorgio's mouth broke into a slow smile. She knew what he was going to do before he clamped a hand on her arm and forced her to walk out of the bathroom in front of him.

"Great minds must think alike, cousin. Ms. Hamilton has a little surprise of her own for you, too."

Dimitrios, dressed in a formal black tux, stood in the

center of the room, his legs slightly apart. When Alex made eye contact with him, he didn't move. There wasn't the slightest flicker of an eyelid or twitch of a muscle.

But as surely as she watched a whiteness creep around his chiseled mouth, as surely as she saw the light extinguished, turning his eyes to black holes, Alex knew everything had changed between them.

She felt her heart die.

Giorgio lifted his palms. "Before you make the mistake of telling me to get out and never darken your doorstep again, you'd better listen to someone who's been lured by Ms. Hamilton's siren song before.

"What I'm attempting to do now, cousin, is save you from yourself. The way you once saved me.

"Of course she was nine years younger then, but well enough aware of her potential to make a play for the youngest Pandakis cousin who couldn't hold his liquor or take his eyes off her during the fashion show. How could I resist her offer of a tour of the silk museum?"

"My grandfather told me to do it as a favor to *your* father!" Alex defended. "That was my job. I received a salary for it. If he'd known you were drunk, he would never have allowed me near you! I didn't know it until you forced me out to the garden." Her voice shook in remembered pain.

"So you say," Giorgio murmured. "Nevertheless we all know how that ended. But what we didn't know at the time was that she would decide to go after her savior. That was you, Dimitrios.

"Only her plan had to be much more cunning because this time she wanted to capture the favorite son."

Alex's eyes closed tightly.

"No more blond hair. A whole new identity. Everything a fait accompli. In the end we were both duped.

"Because you're a man of honor who didn't expose my embarrassing lapse to the family, Dimitrios, I've decided to return the favor. When I leave this room, no one will ever know she almost made a fool of you, too.

"Let us pray that in future, you'll set your sights somewhere other than the Pandakis family, Ms. Hamilton. My brother Vaso tells me the prime minister was very taken with you, even in your altered state. If he could see what I'm looking at right now, you would end up his pillow friend."

Blind with fury, Alex slapped him hard across the face. It was something she'd been wanting to do for nine years. He put his hand to the place where she could already see red.

"Cousin." He nodded to both of them before leaving the bedroom.

A stunning silence filled the room.

Dimitrios's wintry regard froze the blood in her veins.

"Please— If you'll just give me a chance, I can explain everything."

"No explanation is needed. I'll be waiting for you in the car. Don't take too long."

She was shaking so hard, she felt faint. Her body broke out in a cold sweat. Then a salty taste filled her mouth. "I—I couldn't go anywhere right now."

Alex reached the bathroom in time to lose her lunch.

She felt his presence in the doorway. After everything else, this was a humiliation beyond enduring.

"I'll send Serilda to you. Have your desk cleaned out by the time I get back to New York on Wednesday.

Charlene will give you an envelope containing your bonus and severance pay."

"Uncle? What are you doing up here on this peak with me?"

They were both sitting against one of the ruins of the castle, looking out over the forest.

Dimitrios bit down on a blade of sweet grass. "I thought it was obvious."

"It might be, except for the fact that you're in love with Alexandra. She should be the one here with you. For that matter, the trade fair's still going on."

"Today was the last day. Vaso's in charge. Stavros can handle any unforeseen problems."

"You mean Alexandra, don't you?"

His eyes closed tightly. *Lord,* the pain.

"No," he finally murmured. "I've relieved her of all responsibilities."

As the words sank in, Leon's head turned sharply in his direction. His brows formed a black bar. "She couldn't have turned down your marriage proposal!"

"She didn't get one," he ground out.

Leon leaped to his feet. His hands went to his hips. He stared at his uncle. "Good grief, you didn't fire her—"

"As a matter of fact I did. By now I presume she's on her way back to New York."

His nephew shook his head. "I only have one question. Why?"

"I don't want to talk about it."

"Then why did you drag me up here?" His nephew sounded angry. It surprised him.

"I wanted you to understand why this place was so important to your father and me."

"But you could have done that anytime!" Leon declared. His mild-mannered nephew seemed to have disappeared. "Why don't you just admit that for once in your life you need someone to confide in?"

Now it was Dimitrios who got to his feet, anxious to change the subject. They'd been up here long enough. It was time to get back to the lodge for the night.

His nephew faced him without blinking. "It's funny, you know? All my life you've been there to listen to my problems, yet you never tell me yours."

"Leon—"

"It's true!" he defended. Color filled his cheeks. "You say you want me around, that you'd like me to go into business with you. But if you can't open up to me about the woman you love, then there's not much point to anything, is there?"

He walked off with the binoculars to study some raptors circling overhead. As Dimitrios watched his long legs eat up the distance, it began to dawn on him that his nephew might just have told him something he'd been longing to hear.

"Alexandra lied to me."

Leon remained where he was. "If she did, she must have had a damn good reason."

Dimitrios followed him, puzzled by Leon's fierce defense of her. "When she applied for a job with the company in New York four years ago, she presented herself as a dowdy, thirty-year-old woman who had brown hair. In reality…"

Images of her curvaceous body and long slender legs barely covered by the towel flashed before his eyes. She was so gorgeous he could hardly breathe when he pictured her in his mind.

"Yes? In reality, what?"

Dimitrios rubbed his chest absently. "She's a green-eyed twenty-five-year-old with long blond hair."

After a moment Leon looked over his shoulder. There was a trace of a smile on his lips. "Really. Since when is that a sin?"

"It's not. But to live with the lie this long *is*."

"Alexandra's a smart woman. No doubt she wanted to look efficient enough to get hired. I doubt she would have gotten past Mrs. Landau if she'd been a knockout." Leon cocked his head. "Is she?"

He knew what his nephew was asking. "She's incredible."

"So what's really wrong? You don't fire the woman who's become your right hand because she's younger than you thought, *and* beautiful."

His nephew's shrewd analysis jolted him.

"You do when you find out she had a plan to trick me into marriage as far back as nine years ago."

"Now we're getting somewhere. You two met nine years ago? How?"

Dimitrios only hesitated a moment, then he recounted the details of that night in New Jersey.

Leon's face lit up. "Forget Giorgio and anything he had to say. She's been in love with *you* all this time. If a woman ever loved me that much, I'd be the happiest man alive."

Maybe they were talking at cross purposes. "Isn't that a bit ironic coming from you?"

"What do you mean?"

"You're planning to enter a monastery."

"I've changed my mind about that, Uncle. This last trip with the guys made me realize I'm more into religious art than religion. That business you talked about? I was thinking that if I finished my studies, we could start a company that manufactured religious artifacts.

"I was talking with some vendors at the fair. They claim there's a huge international market out there for them if they could find the right distributor."

By tacit agreement they started down the peak. Dimitrios let his nephew chat away. It was like hearing beautiful music after a cacophony of sounds.

Talking with Leon about Alexandra had at least brought him out of his near comatose state. Unfortunately there were things his nephew still didn't know. Things Dimitrios could never tell him without painting Ananke in a bad light.

"Have you told your mother the news?"

"As soon as we get home tomorrow."

A groan came out of Dimitrios. Without Alexandra, he had no idea how he was going to get through the night, let alone tomorrow. He didn't even want to think about the rest of his life.

CHAPTER TEN

IT WAS after ten p.m. when Alex drove the rental car into the parking area of the Dadia lodge. With Michael's help they'd found a hairdresser who could speak English. He followed Michael's directions to put her hair back to its normal blond color.

The appointment had taken hours. Then she'd bought some new clothes, including the khaki shorts and white knit top she was wearing. That barely left enough time to make the last flight to Alexandropoulos.

Dimitrios had ordered her back to New York, but she couldn't leave Greece until she'd spent a day in the forest where she'd known joy with him. It was her own way of saying goodbye to her dreams.

She didn't have a reservation, but she'd decided to use Dimitrios's name just one more time. If that didn't work, then she'd stay in the parking lot and sleep in the car all night.

Tomorrow morning she'd hike the trail to the observatory. She could be up and down the mountain in time to get a flight back to Thessalonica. Once at the airport, she'd switch terminals for her overseas flight to New York.

When she went inside the office, there was no one at the counter. She tapped the bell with the palm of her hand. In a minute the concierge who'd waited on them before came out from the dining room area.

He nodded to her, but there was no sign of recognition.

It was like being reborn in a different skin. Before she could ask, he waved his hand back and forth. "No rooms. All is full for the fair."

"I'm Alexandra Hamilton, Kyrie Dimitrios Pandakis's secretary? I came with him a few days ago?"

That perked him up. "Yes? One moment, please." He reached for the phone receiver to talk to someone in Greek.

Thank heaven her plan had worked. She desperately needed a bed. After sobbing all night, then going hard all day, Alex was so exhausted she was ready to drop.

He put the receiver back on the hook. "If you will wait five minutes, your room will be ready."

"Thank you very much. Let me pay you now."

"That is all right. It is already taken care of."

"But I insist on paying." She signed two one-hundred-dollar traveler's checks and left them on the counter.

He nodded again. "Here is your key. The room is number twenty on the far end."

"I'll find it."

She got back in the car and drove past the other cottages until she came to the last one. Relieved there was a light on inside the room, she climbed out of the car and removed her suitcase from the back seat.

Lugging it to the door, she inserted the key and let herself inside, dragging the suitcase behind her. She nudged the door shut with her hip.

That's when she saw the man who'd haunted her dreams for so many years emerge from the bathroom wearing nothing but a pair of low-slung navy sweats.

"I don't believe it," she whispered in shock.

Their gazes fused as if a sizzling bolt of electricity connected them.

He'd thought he'd seen the last of her!

Zeus had banished her to the nethermost regions of the universe, yet here she was back again at the foot of Olympus, his favorite place, using his name to gain entrance, no less.

"Some coincidences defy every known law," she began in an unsteady voice. "I wouldn't blame you if you thought I'd charged the room to your account. If you'll call the concierge, he'll tell you I left money for the room on the counter. Forgive me for intruding."

Alex had to get out of there. But when she turned to go, Dimitrios had reached the door ahead of her, preventing her from leaving. She had no idea anyone could move that fast.

After locking the door, he picked up her suitcase like it was full of air and put it on the extra bed. When he turned out the light, only the soft glow from the bedside lamp remained.

She backed away to one of the other twin beds and sat down on the end of it. In truth, her legs would no longer support her.

He came closer, his fists on his hips. Since she'd been in Greece she'd seen several statues of Zeus standing in that exact position, his magnificent body nude except for a drape.

That's how she thought of Dimitrios. A man who was more than a man. Bigger than life.

"How long did you plan to continue being someone you're not? No more lies, Alexandra." His voice seemed to come from a dark, deep cavern.

"You would have known everything if Leon hadn't come in your bedroom the other night."

His intake of breath sounded like ripping silk. Distracted by the stunning virility of his body, she lowered her eyes. *To think a mortal man could look like that!*

"Leon's not here now. Let's have it all, then be done with it."

Her head was still averted. "Everything your cousin accused me of was true except for one thing. I was a pretty naïve sixteen-year-old who wouldn't have known how to attract an older man if I'd tried.

"But there is one thing I do remember about that night. It was the deep disappointment I felt when my grandfather asked me to escort Giorgio around the museum instead of you. Your cousin probably sensed it. Maybe that's what set him off."

To Alex's wonderment he said, "It wouldn't have taken much. You were the most beautiful of your sisters, even back then. With your long golden hair, you were exceptionally appealing to a family of dark-haired men. All my cousins commented on you during the fashion show.

"In fairness to Giorgio, one could forgive him for being enchanted. But everything else that happened that night was criminal. I saw him go off with you and sensed there could be trouble. When too much time lapsed without your reappearance, I went to look for you."

Alex's body shook convulsively. "What if you hadn't come?"

A sound of exasperation escaped his throat, permeating the room. She didn't know if it poured from pure anger or frustration, or both. Suddenly Dimitrios was sitting next to her, his hand sliding beneath her hair to the nape of her neck.

"I blame myself for that night," he murmured, stroking her skin to gentle her. "I'd known for a while he was an alcoholic. He had no business being around you in that condition.

"When I got him back to the hotel, I waited until he'd sobered up, then I threatened to expose him to his father.

"Giorgio knew what that would mean. Uncle Spiros put the fear in everyone. He would have disowned Giorgio had he known the truth. We made a pact that night. If he never went near alcohol again, I'd never tell my uncle. To my cousin's credit, he got help and left it alone."

"But he's so jealous of you it's painful to hear him talk."

His fingers tangled in her hair. "I know. It's been a burden I wouldn't wish on my worst enemy."

Moisture stung her eyes. "It's because you're so wonderful. There's no one to match you, Dimitrios. I love you so much," she blurted. "But I was wrong to deceive you."

"Why did you?" He got up from the bed, leaving her desolate. "If you wanted a job with me so badly, why weren't you straightforward? You could have passed on your grandfather's name through Mrs. Landau. I would have remembered and given you a personal interview."

She clasped her hands. "I know that now. But at the time I thought I'd have a better chance if I toned down my appearearance so Mrs. Landau would consider me for a job. Michael helped me, and I was hired. Mrs. Landau was so good to me, I couldn't admit to her what I'd done. After she had that heart attack, I wanted to tell you everything. I swear it. But you were so upset about her passing, I thought I'd wait a while. Unfortunately no time ever seemed right.

"Dimitrios?" she whispered in anguish. "The thing I feel worst about is destroying the trust you had in me. Without it, there's nothing!"

"Exactly."

What did he mean? She wiped her eyes. "Are you going to let what I've done prevent you from having faith in a woman's love?"

"Does it matter?" He lay down on the other bed.

"What happened to hurt you so deeply?" Without conscious thought she moved to the other bed and sat down next to him.

"Please, Dimitrios—" Her voice throbbed. As if it had a life of its own, her hand reached out to touch him where she could feel his heart pounding. "Tell me who did this to you."

His great body shook. "One night when I was twelve, I heard my brother in the hall of Uncle Spiros's villa. He was stealing away to get married to Ananke because she was pregnant with his child. At that moment, I *hated* her."

Alex was listening, trying with all her heart to understand. "Of course you did, darling. He was your whole world and she was taking him away from you." Poor Ananke had borne a burden she knew nothing about.

Dimitrios grasped her hand so hard it hurt, but he wasn't aware of the pressure. His thoughts were somewhere else.

"It was more than that. He said she didn't love him. He said she'd gotten pregnant on purpose so she could become a member of the Pandakis family. I begged him not to marry Ananke if she didn't love him, but he said he had to. It was a matter of honor." His body went taut.

They were close to the truth now, but she sensed there was still more to come. "What else did he say?"

"He said our mother probably married our father for the same reason."

Groaning with sorrow for the heartbroken boy inside the man, she waited for the rest.

"Leonides warned me that one day many women would come after me for my money. They would try to trick me into marriage by getting pregnant with my child."

How cruel his brother had been to disillusion a vulnerable boy.

"And what did you say?"

"I told him that would never happen to me because I would never make love to a woman before I married her."

Alex's thoughts reeled as she considered all the women Dimitrios had ever known or been with.

Her heart caught in her throat. "Did you keep your vow?" *Was it possible?*

His chest rose and fell. "Yes. It was easy. No woman ever tempted me beyond my power to resist. I was so pleased with myself, I didn't realize my secretary had stolen my heart."

At last Alex expelled the breath she'd been holding.

"Oh, darling—" She buried her face in his luxuriant hair. "I can't believe that out of all the beautiful women you've known, you would be tempted by a non descript little nobody like me."

"Brown haired or blond, there's nothing non descript about you, Alexandra." He pulled her to him. His hands started to roam over her body, finding every line and curve. "When you nursed me through the night and stroked the hair off my forehead, that vow was the last thing on my mind. If Leon hadn't interrupted us, you could be pregnant with my child right now. You don't know how hard it was trying not to drag you into my bed."

She kissed the corner of his mouth, delirious with longing for her first taste of him. "Then I might have been tempted to break my vow, too."

His hands stilled, then suddenly their positions were reversed. Dimitrios gazed down into her eyes. "You made the same vow?" His voice sounded husky.

"When you saved me at sixteen, you won everything I have to give, what I'm dying to give. I'm so in love with you," she cried. "Nine years has been too long to wait. Kiss me, Kyrie Pandakis. Love me," she begged.

"Agape mou."

The Greek endearment was smothered as his mouth descended on hers with primitive hunger. On fire after such long-suppressed passion, they sought to absorb the very essence of each other.

This was ecstasy. She couldn't stop moaning from the pleasure pain of being in his arms like this at last.

Their legs tangled until Alex was trapped right where she'd always wanted to be. Her heart streamed into his until it felt like they'd always been connected.

She'd dreamed about loving him like this, but to finally be the participant in a love match with her real-life Zeus was wonderful beyond bearing.

"I'm ready to eat you alive," he confessed on a ragged breath after they'd been devouring each other over and over again. Their passion knew no bounds.

"I've been ready for that much much longer than you can imagine. You're my addiction. If I had my way, we would never leave this room again."

"It's your choice whether we wear white at our wedding tomorrow morning."

Alex groaned. "That wasn't fair to propose marriage and abstinence in the same breath." She covered his neck and powerful shoulders with feverish kisses. "Now I understand why the opposition runs when they see you coming. No one drives a harder bargain."

Laughter rumbled out of him as he buried his face in her golden hair splayed across the pillow.

"Are we really getting married tomorrow?"

He smoothed some gleaming strands of hair off her forehead. "I must have said something to please you. I can see your gorgeous green eyes shimmering."

"I wish we were man and wife already."

"You think I don't?" he came back on an almost savage note. "I've arranged for a special permit. If the priest were willing, we'd be in that little church down the road saying our vows this very minute. As it is, Leon is in Dadia right now making all the arrangements."

"Leon's here?"

Dimitrios cupped the back of her head and kissed her long and hard before finally letting her go again. He sounded out of breath.

"After I left your bedroom, my state of mind was so black, I had to get out of the villa. I dragged him with me. We flew here. Today I forced him up to the top of the peak with me.

"It was an illuminating experience for our roles to be reversed. After he informed me that being with Michael and his friends convinced him he doesn't want the life of a religious after all—''

''Dimitrios—''

He smiled at her joyous outburst. ''He demanded that I tell him what was wrong with me. One thing led to another, and it all came out.''

''I love that nephew of yours more every day.''

Dimitrios kissed every feature of her upturned face. ''He's crazy about you, too. While I was showering earlier, the phone rang in our room. Leon answered it. The concierge told him my secretary had arrived and was asking for a room. My nephew took it upon himself to tell the man to give you a key.

''When I came out of the bathroom, Leon was on his way out the front door with the rental car keys. I asked him what was going on. A smile lit up his face. He said he was sleeping in Dadia for the night because my future bride would be entering the room any second now.

''Before he shut the door, he added that he would call on the local priest to arrange a wedding. He'll return tomorrow complete with the clothes we'll be married in.''

Overjoyed, Alex threw her arms around his neck. ''When the priest finds out he's been given the honor of marrying the most revered man in all Greece, he won't let anything stand in the way. Now I know it's really going to happen! I'm so excited. Dance with me, Kyrie.''

''Now?''

''Yes. Like we did the other night.''

''I prefer you right where you are.''

''So do I, but dancing's safer.''

''Really,'' he said in a devilish voice.

She rolled off the bed to turn on the lamp. After she'd

flipped on the radio to a music station, she looked back at him.

Her eyes widened as he levered himself off the bed. All six foot three inches of him were hard-packed muscle. With his black hair tousled and those black eyes glowing like hot coals, she really couldn't catch her breath.

"Have I ever told you what a sensational looking man you are? It's a shame you can't go around in your sweats all the time."

His white smile robbed her of breath.

"That's the difference between a man and a woman. I'm looking forward to watching you run around in nothing at all. But right now I'll settle for what the gods have dropped in my lap tonight.

"Come here to me, you beautiful creature. I need to hold you," he said in an aching voice. He began dancing and held out his arms. Alex ran into them.

"I'm so happy, I'm afraid I might have a heart attack before morning and then I'll never know what it's like to—"

Dimitrios stopped moving because his body was riddled with laughter. He rocked her back and forth.

"Oh, Alexandra. Life with you is one continual gift."

"I hope so. The thing is, what if I don't know how— I mean—"

He chuckled harder. "We'll learn together." He pivoted her around the room. "We'll have children together. We'll do it all, my love."

Her eyes closed tightly. "I love the sound of that. But do you suppose there's a lot more to it than we realize?"

"If there is, we have the rest of our lives to find out."

She threw her head back as he spun her around. "Morning, noon and night."

His lips twitched. "I hear that's a rather exhausting schedule for the husband on a regular basis."

"Why not the wife?"

"I don't know." He pulled her close. Growling into her neck he said, "I guess that's something else we're going to find out."

She stared up at him with stars in her eyes. "It's thrilling, isn't it. Tomorrow we're going to go where neither of us has gone before."

He whirled them to a stop. "With you, everything is thrilling." Then his handsome face sobered.

"I would never have wished the experience with Giorgio on you, but—"

"I know." She kissed his lips quiet. "I'd like to think it was all meant to be. He stopped drinking and turned his life around."

Dimitrios nodded.

"You and I are so lucky, we can afford to be kind to him."

He crushed her in his arms. "I tremble to imagine my life without you."

"I don't even want to think about it." She clung to him. "Darling? Ananke has suffered, too. Did it ever occur to you that she might have loved your brother the way I loved you in the beginning? Especially if Leonides was as handsome as my husband-to-be," she whispered in his ear before biting his lobe gently. "You Pandakis men make an enormous impact on the female population, you know."

He sculpted the back of her head with his hand. "I

hadn't thought about it before, but I'm thinking hard now. Leonides slept with her because he wanted to.''

"That's right, and they got caught. It happens to lovers every day. At that point he was down on all women. Maybe even your mother?''

"You're reading my mind again." He drew her over to the bed and lay down next to her. Pulling her close, his mouth roved her face, kissing every square inch. "There's something I need to do before this night is over.''

"What?'' She'd settled against him and didn't want to move again.

"Call your parents and ask them if it's all right that I'm stealing you away. If they want to see us married, we can always fly to Paterson and say our vows again in front of all your friends and family.''

Alex just kept finding more reasons to love him. "Mom and Dad won't believe I finally got my heart's desire. You're going to make them so happy. I've been their most worrisome child.''

The bed shook with his laughter. He'd been doing a lot of that. It was a glorious sound. Almost as glorious as hearing him call out her name after he'd fallen asleep in her arms. The longing in his voice made her heart leap. He couldn't wait for morning, either.

EPILOGUE

THERE was a rap on the cottage door. "Alexandra? It's Leon. I hope you're ready because Uncle Dimitrios is a nervous wreck. If we don't appear at the church in five minutes, he's going to charge back here to find out what's wrong."

"Just a minute!"

Alex could scarcely credit that a few days ago she'd been in pain watching another wedding celebration in a nearby meadow. With Dimitrios standing behind her, she'd wished with all her heart she'd been that ecstatic bride dancing in her new husband's arms.

Now, miraculously, this was her wedding day. Leon had come to escort her to the beautiful little forest church where she was about to be married to the man she loved more than life itself. Alex was so euphoric, she could hardly breathe.

After making an adjustment of the garland in her hair, she gave herself a final glance in the mirror. The white wedding dress Leon had purchased in the village fit her perfectly.

"Alexandra?"

"I'm coming!"

She hurried through the cottage and opened the door. To her joy, Leon had brought someone familiar with him.

"Michael!"

He took a step backward and put up his arms up as if to ward off her radiance.

"Oh, stop!"

He batted his eyelids like he did at the salon. "After four years, you've burst forth from your brown chrysalis. My eyes need time to adjust to your beauty."

"I'm so glad you're here!" she cried before giving him a big hug.

Leon looked on with a wide smile. "My uncle thought you would like someone from home to be here for you."

Dimitrios understood her better than she understood herself. Her love for him knew no bounds.

"Tsk, tsk. No tears today, darling," Michael admonished.

Leon opened the passenger door of his rental car for her. "I suggest we get going, otherwise I refuse to be responsible for the consequences. My uncle's never been in love before. I have a feeling my life won't be worth a drachma if we keep him in suspense any longer."

Alex didn't want to spend another second apart from Dimitrios, either. Two hours before, he'd left with Leon to make final preparations and allow her time to get ready. It had felt like three years.

Michael helped her into the car, then climbed in the back while Leon drove. The church was only a mile down the road. There was an air of unreality about the whole thing as they pulled into the parking area. Except for two cars, it looked deserted.

A hot sun shone directly overhead. Through the pines, rays fell on the exterior of the charming white church, making it glisten.

While Michael accompanied her to the entrance, Leon snapped pictures. Thankful he'd thought of a camera, she realized how important it was to preserve this day for posterity, especially photographs of her gorgeous husband.

"I guess I don't need to ask if you're ready to take this momentous step," Michael murmured.

"No," she answered in a tremulous voice.

He kissed her cheek. "Promise to come down from Olympus once in a while to pay this mortal a visit?"

"You know I will!" she cried softly.

Leon joined them on the steps. "Shall we go in and make my uncle a happy man?"

"Relax, Dimitrios," Stavros admonished. "They've arrived. Turn around and see what your nephew has brought you."

With heart thudding, Dimitrios spun on his heel in time to see Alexandra hurrying toward him with Michael holding her arm and Leon taking up the rear.

The priest broke off his conversation with Stavros's wife and Ananke in order to greet Dimitrios' bride-to-be.

She looked a vision of gold and white.

Almost suffocating with the need to love her into oblivion, he had to hold back a little longer while the priest led her forward and placed her right hand over Dimitrios's left.

Her green eyes glowed with a new light. "Darling," she whispered, out of breath, squeezing his fingers. He could feel her love like a living thing.

"You won't understand what the priest is saying," he murmured. "Just realize that when it's over, you'll be my wife."

"And you'll be my husband. It's all I've ever wanted." Her voice caught.

Dimitrios knew better than most men how much and how long he'd been loved by this woman. Humbled to be given such a gift, he was glad he'd kept his vow all these years. It was his gift to her.

After kissing the back of her hand, he nodded to the priest to start the ceremony.

The women were positioned beside Alexandra. Leon took his place next to Dimitrios, followed by Stavros, then Michael.

The priest smiled at them, then began the age-old ritual. Dimitrios couldn't help but reflect on his brother's marriage, performed by a priest in the dead of night with only Ananke's grandmother to look on.

That was an unhappy time, but it belonged to the past.

When it came time for him to slide the gold wedding band on Alexandra's ring finger, she smiled up at him with her heart in her eyes. The beautiful face lifted to his represented his present and his future, bringing him ineffable joy.

To think today was only the beginning.

From boardroom…to bride and groom!

A secret romance, a forbidden affair, a thrilling
attraction…where a date in the office diary leads to
an appointment at the altar!

Sometimes a "9 to 5" relationship continues
after hours in these tantalizing office
romances…with a difference!

Look out for some of your favorite

Harlequin Romance®

authors, including:

JESSICA HART: Assignment: Baby
(February 2002, #3688)

BARBARA McMAHON: His Secretary's Secret
(April 2002, #3698)

LEIGH MICHAELS: The Boss's Daughter
(August 2002, #3711)

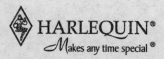

HARLEQUIN®
Makes any time special ®

Visit us at www.eHarlequin.com

HR9T05

MONTANA *Born*

From the bestselling series

MONTANA MAVERICKS

Wed in Whitehorn

Two tales that capture living and loving
beneath the Big Sky.

THE MARRIAGE MAKER by Christie Ridgway

Successful businessman Ethan Redford never proposed a deal he
couldn't close—and that included marriage to Cleo Kincaid Monroe!

AND THE WINNER...WEDS! by Robin Wells

Prim and proper Frannie Hannon yearned for Austin Parker, but
her pearls and sweater sets couldn't catch his boots and jeans—or
could they?

And don't miss

MONTANA *Bred*

Featuring

JUST PRETENDING by Myrna Mackenzie

&

STORMING WHITEHORN by Christine Scott

Available in May 2002
Available only from Silhouette at your favorite retail outlet.

Silhouette
Where love comes alive.

Visit Silhouette at www.eHarlequin.com   PSBORN

This Mother's Day
Give Your Mom
 A Royal Treat

Win a fabulous one-week vacation in
Puerto Rico for you and your mother at
the luxurious Inter-Continental San Juan
Resort & Casino. The prize includes round
trip airfare for two, breakfast daily and a
mother and daughter day of beauty
at the beachfront hotel's spa.

INTER·CONTINENTAL
San Juan
RESORT & CASINO

Here's all you have to do:

Tell us in 100 words or less how your
mother helped with the romance in your
life. It may be a story about your engagement,
wedding or those boyfriends when you were
a teenager or any other romantic advice
from your mother. The entry will be judged
based on its originality, emotionally
compelling nature and sincerity.
See official rules on following page.

Send your entry to:
Mother's Day Contest

In Canada
P.O. Box 637
Fort Erie, Ontario
L2A 5X3

In U.S.A.
P.O. Box 9076
3010 Walden Ave.
Buffalo, NY
14269-9076

Or enter online at www.eHarlequin.com

All entries must be postmarked by April 1, 2002.
Winner will be announced May 1, 2002. Contest open to
Canadian and U.S. residents who are 18 years of age and older.
No purchase necessary to enter. Void where prohibited.

PRROY

HARLEQUIN MOTHER'S DAY CONTEST 2216
OFFICIAL RULES
NO PURCHASE NECESSARY TO ENTER

Two ways to enter:

• **Via The Internet:** Log on to the Harlequin romance website (www.eHarlequin.com) anytime beginning 12:01 a.m. E.S.T., January 1, 2002 through 11:59 p.m. E.S.T., April 1, 2002 and follow the directions displayed on-line to enter your name, address (including zip code), e-mail address and in 100 words or fewer, describe how your mother helped with the romance in your life.

• **Via Mail:** Handprint (or type) on an 8 1/2" x 11" plain piece of paper, your name, address (including zip code) and e-mail address (if you have one), and in 100 words or fewer, describe how your mother helped with the romance in your life. Mail your entry via first-class mail to: Harlequin Mother's Day Contest 2216, (in the U.S.) P.O. Box 9076, Buffalo, NY 14269-9076; (in Canada) P.O. Box 637, Fort Erie, Ontario, Canada L2A 5X3.

For eligibility, entries must be submitted either through a completed Internet transmission or postmarked no later than 11:59 p.m. E.S.T., April 1, 2002 (mail-in entries must be received by April 9, 2002). Limit one entry per person, household address and e-mail address. On-line and/or mailed entries received from persons residing in geographic areas in which entry is not permissible will be disqualified.

Entries will be judged by a panel of judges, consisting of members of the Harlequin editorial, marketing and public relations staff using the following criteria:
  • Originality - 50%
  • Emotional Appeal - 25%
  • Sincerity - 25%

In the event of a tie, duplicate prizes will be awarded. Decisions of the judges are final.

Prize: A 6-night/7-day stay for two at the Inter-Continental San Juan Resort & Casino, including round-trip coach air transportation from gateway airport nearest winner's home (approximate retail value: $4,000). Prize includes breakfast daily and a mother and daughter day of beauty at the beachfront hotel's spa. Prize consists of only those items listed as part of the prize. Prize is valued in U.S. currency.

All entries become the property of Torstar Corp. and will not be returned. No responsibility is assumed for lost, late, illegible, incomplete, inaccurate, non-delivered or misdirected mail or misdirected e-mail, for technical, hardware or software failures of any kind, lost or unavailable network connections, or failed, incomplete, garbled or delayed computer transmission or any human error which may occur in the receipt or processing of the entries in this Contest.

Contest open only to residents of the U.S. (except Colorado) and Canada, who are 18 years of age or older and is void wherever prohibited by law; all applicable laws and regulations apply. Any litigation within the Province of Quebec respecting the conduct or organization of a publicity contest may be submitted to the Régie des alcools, des courses et des jeux for a ruling. Any litigation respecting the awarding of a prize may be submitted to the Régie des alcools, des courses et des jeux only for the purpose of helping the parties reach a settlement. Employees and immediate family members of Torstar Corp. and D.L. Blair, Inc., their affiliates, subsidiaries and all other agencies, entities and persons connected with the use, marketing or conduct of this Contest are not eligible to enter. Taxes on prize are the sole responsibility of winner. Acceptance of any prize offered constitutes permission to use winner's name, photograph or other likeness for the purposes of advertising, trade and promotion on behalf of Torstar Corp., its affiliates and subsidiaries without further compensation to the winner, unless prohibited by law.

Winner will be determined no later than April 15, 2002 and be notified by mail. Winner will be required to sign and return an Affidavit of Eligibility form within 15 days after winner notification. Non-compliance within that time period may result in disqualification and an alternate winner may be selected. Winner of trip must execute a Release of Liability prior to ticketing and must possess required travel documents (e.g. Passport, photo ID) where applicable. Travel must be completed within 12 months of selection and is subject to traveling companion completing and returning a Release of Liability prior to travel; and hotel and flight accommodations availability. Certain restrictions and blockout dates may apply. No substitution of prize permitted by winner. Torstar Corp. and D.L. Blair, Inc., their parents, affiliates, and subsidiaries are not responsible for errors in printing or electronic presentation of Contest, or entries. In the event of printing or other errors which may result in unintended prize values or duplication of prizes, all affected entries shall be null and void. If for any reason the Internet portion of the Contest is not capable of running as planned, including infection by computer virus, bugs, tampering, unauthorized intervention, fraud, technical failures, or any other causes beyond the control of Torstar Corp. which corrupt or affect the administration, secrecy, fairness, integrity or proper conduct of the Contest, Torstar Corp. reserves the right, at its sole discretion, to disqualify any individual who tampers with the entry process and to cancel, terminate, modify or suspend the Contest or the Internet portion thereof. In the event the Internet portion must be terminated a notice will be posted on the website and all entries received prior to termination will be judged in accordance with these rules. In the event of a dispute regarding an on-line entry, the entry will be deemed submitted by the authorized holder of the e-mail account submitted at the time of entry. Authorized account holder is defined as the natural person who is assigned to an e-mail address by an Internet access provider, on-line service provider or other organization that is responsible for arranging e-mail address for the domain associated with the submitted e-mail address. Torstar Corp. and/or D.L. Blair Inc. assumes no responsibility for any computer injury or damage related to or resulting from accessing and/or downloading any sweepstakes material. Rules are subject to any requirements/limitations imposed by the FCC. **Purchase or acceptance of a product offer does not improve your chances of winning.**

For winner's name (available after May 1, 2002), send a self-addressed, stamped envelope to: Harlequin Mother's Day Contest Winners 2216, P.O. Box 4200 Blair, NE 68009-4200 or you may access the www.eHarlequin.com Web site through June 3, 2002.

Contest sponsored by Torstar Corp., P.O. Box 9042, Buffalo, NY 14269-9042.

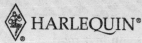